Smg

W9-BXV-442

Something was bothering Tyler as he grabbed Dusty's leash.

The K-9 was up, alive with excitement. Tyler laughed at Dusty's exuberance, but still there was the nagging detail deep down in his gut that refused to surface.

What was it?

He hastened toward the conference room where Penny had gone. As they got closer, Dusty's nose quivered. Two more steps and she pulled on the leash, eager to get to the scent. An old one. One she'd remembered from before.

The scent left by Randall Gage and his black marker.

"Penny," Tyler shouted as he ran. "Don't open that box!"

TRUE BLUE K-9 UNIT: BROOKLYN

These police officers fight for justice
with the help of their brave canine partners.

Copycat Killer by Laura Scott, April 2020
Chasing Secrets by Heather Woodhaven, May 2020
Deadly Connection by Lenora Worth, June 2020
Explosive Situation by Terri Reed, July 2020
Tracking a Kidnapper by Valerie Hansen, August 2020
Scene of the Crime by Sharon Dunn, September 2020
Cold Case Pursuit by Dana Mentink, October 2020
Delayed Justice by Shirlee McCoy, November 2020
True Blue K-9 Unit: Brooklyn Christmas by Laura Scott and Maggie K. Black, December 2020

Dana Mentink is a national bestselling author. She has been honored to win two Carol Awards, a HOLT Medallion and an RT Reviewers' Choice Best Book Award. She's authored more than thirty novels to date for Love Inspired Suspense and Harlequin Heartwarming. Dana loves feedback from her readers. Contact her at danamentink.com.

Books by Dana Mentink

Love Inspired Suspense

True Blue K-9 Unit: Brooklyn

Cold Case Pursuit

True Blue K-9 Unit

Shield of Protection
Act of Valor

Roughwater Ranch Cowboys

Danger on the Ranch
Deadly Christmas Pretense
Cold Case Connection
Secrets Resurfaced

Gold Country Cowboys

Cowboy Christmas Guardian
Treacherous Trails
Cowboy Bodyguard
Lost Christmas Memories

Visit the Author Profile page at Harlequin.com for more titles.

Cold Case Pursuit

Dana Mentink

LOVE INSPIRED SUSPENSE
INSPIRATIONAL ROMANCE

If you purchased this book without a cover you should be aware that this book is stolen property. It was reported as "unsold and destroyed" to the publisher, and neither the author nor the publisher has received any payment for this "stripped book."

Special thanks and acknowledgment are given to Dana Mentink for her contribution to the True Blue K-9 Unit: Brooklyn miniseries.

LOVE INSPIRED® SUSPENSE
INSPIRATIONAL ROMANCE

Recycling programs for this product may not exist in your area.

ISBN-13: 978-1-335-57466-4

Cold Case Pursuit

Copyright © 2020 by Harlequin Books S.A.

All rights reserved. No part of this book may be used or reproduced in any manner whatsoever without written permission except in the case of brief quotations embodied in critical articles and reviews.

This is a work of fiction. Names, characters, places and incidents are either the product of the author's imagination or are used fictitiously. Any resemblance to actual persons, living or dead, businesses, companies, events or locales is entirely coincidental.

This edition published by arrangement with Harlequin Books S.A.

For questions and comments about the quality of this book, please contact us at CustomerService@Harlequin.com.

Love Inspired
22 Adelaide St. West, 40th Floor
Toronto, Ontario M5H 4E3, Canada
www.Harlequin.com

Printed in U.S.A.

Brethren, I count not myself to have apprehended:
but this one thing I do, forgetting those things
which are behind, and reaching forth unto those things
which are before, I press toward the mark for the prize
of the high calling of God in Christ Jesus.

—*Philippians* 3:13–14

To my precious dog-loving reader friends...
thank you for your kindness and support!

ONE

Penelope McGregor shivered at the distant creak from the back of the house. Goose bumps erupted along her spine. Just the aged floorboards swelling from the falling October temperatures. It was as if the old Brooklyn home struggled under the weight of a new day. Penny knew the feeling.

She forced her attention back to her phone screen, scanning the party supplies. An image appeared and her lungs constricted, overcome by the crushing weight of terror. It was as if she'd fallen into a pit of ice that was freezing her breath away, one gasp at a time. The picture of the blue-haired clown mask leered at her, the mouth agape like a crimson wound.

It's just a picture. It's not real.

But it was as if she was four years old again, standing in the dingy kitchen, watching the blood pooling around the bodies of her parents while a man in a blue-haired clown mask stared down at her.

He'd leaned close, all those years ago, close enough for her to smell the tobacco on his breath. His voice was strange and muffled through the mask as he handed her a stuffed monkey. And in her childish confusion, she'd taken it, stunned at the sight of the blood and the terrible stillness of her mother and father. Too frightened to speak, too terrified to scream.

Annoyed with herself, she clicked the website closed. She'd been looking for inspiration for the October open house at the station. She wanted to make it a fun event for the police families at the Brooklyn K-9 Unit, the NYPD offshoot in Bay Ridge where she proudly served as the desk clerk and self-appointed morale officer. The muscles in her stomach remained tight, her ears still straining against the quiet of the Sheepshead Bay home she shared with her cop brother, Bradley, and his K-9 partner, King.

Lately she had been double-checking door locks, troubled by noises at night that kept her awake. She wanted to believe it was paranoia, but deep down she knew that the nightmare was coming to life again. She'd known it since she'd received the text from the man who'd slaughtered her parents. The text had been anonymous, sent from an untraceable number, but that hardly mattered. Even though the tech gurus at headquarters hadn't been able to pinpoint where the message had originated, she knew exactly who'd sent it last month, twenty years and six months after the murders.

Randall Gage, the killer clown.

She pictured him typing out the message, face hidden behind that horrible mask, except for his green eyes.

It was a mistake to let you live.

You first, then your brother, his text had promised.

Thanks to US Marshal Emmett Gage, Randall's cousin, there was finally DNA evidence proving Randall had killed Penny and Bradley's parents. The information had hit the news and caused a media sensation. Officers in the Brooklyn K-9 Unit, including Bradley, all reassured her that it was only a matter of time before Randall Gage was captured. He would never get close enough to hurt her family again, they said, and she tried hard to believe it. The text told her otherwise. For some reason she could not fathom, he was not going to give up until she was dead.

Peering out the window, she was relieved to see a police car driving slowly by for its hourly check. It had taken all her force of will to dissuade her brother from having a cop camped out in the house with her. For twenty years she'd struggled to prove to herself that she was not a helpless victim. She had to try to believe she was safe, in order to refuse Gage any more power over her.

But there was a second person's life hanging in the balance now, as well. Six months earlier, on the twentieth anniversary of the crime, another little girl was given a stuffed monkey by a man in a clown mask. She pictured Lucy Emery, the painfully shy child. How had she felt when she'd seen her own parents lying dead on the floor? Her heart constricted when she thought about Lucy. The two cases were eerily similar—the mask, and the fact that the girl had been neglected by her parents, just as Penny had.

Had Randall Gage made Lucy an orphan, too? Or was a copycat killer at work? As if one deranged clown wasn't enough. The thought of young Lucy just starting the terrible journey that Penny had been walking for the past two decades caused a churning in her stomach. At least Lucy been taken in by her aunt and K-9 cop Nate Slater after the two had married. It was another strange parallel to her own life, since she and Bradley had been adopted by a retired NYPD detective and his darling wife.

Would Lucy get a chance to live free from the shadow of fear? Not until the case was solved and Randall Gage or the copycat killer was behind bars.

The creaking noise whispered from the back of the house, louder now. She willed herself to be still. Seconds ticked by. Nothing but the typical sounds of the two-story house they rented that was tucked between two other family homes. The aging fixtures and the charming wood were part of the reason she and Bradley had chosen the home. The small yard was perfect for King to stretch his legs, too.

Her cell phone rang. She jumped, then answered.

"Hello, Penny. I'm on my way to drive

you to work." Detective Tyler Walker's tone was all business. She could picture the serious blond-haired, blue-eyed cop with his tracking dog, Dusty, by his side. A blush rose to her cheeks. The detective was seven years older than Penelope's twenty-four, but somehow she always felt like he saw her as not much more than a child. That man was six-feet-three inches of no-nonsense grit, emphasis on the *no-nonsense*. His smiles were rare, at least when she was around.

"No need for you to drive me. I can take the train," she said.

"It's no problem. Better for you to ride with me. Bradley is stuck on a case, and he doesn't want you traveling to work alone."

She knew it would do no good to argue. "All right. I'll be ready. I…" She stopped. Had she heard something inside the house? Or was it the wind in the trees outside? She'd already stewed in embarrassed silence when Tyler had scoured the house and yard the day before to find the source of a scratching she'd heard.

"It sounds like someone is trying to break in," she'd told him.

He'd insisted she wait in his squad car while he searched the house. Finally, he'd announced, *"You've got a squirrel on your roof, doing his best to store a pile of acorns in your gutter."*

She'd gone red-hot with mortification.

"Penelope?" Tyler's voice jerked her back to the present. "Everything okay?"

Should she tell him about the sound? But it was just the normal house noises, certainly. No way did she want to embarrass herself a second time in front of him. "Yes. Everything is fine. I'll be ready when you get here."

"All right. See you in fifteen minutes or so." He disconnected.

She'd be safe, with her babysitter Tyler en route. It was embarrassing, humiliating even, to be forced back into the helpless-child role. It was 180 degrees from the person she'd tried be.

Again, a sound in the rear of the old home made her tense. Bradley had told her the swiftly cooling October temperatures wreaked havoc on the ancient pipes. Tyler was on his way. She could call him back and ask him to come inside and check when he arrived, but the thought made her cringe.

Sticking her chin up and squaring her shoulders, she checked each room on the ground floor, Bradley's tiny study, his bedroom, the bathroom and even the hall closet. Her search ended in her bedroom—empty, as she'd known it would be. *You see, you worrywort? Perfectly secure.* Cool autumn air fluttered the blinds.

She stopped dead.

The window was open, the one she'd left closed tight and locked.

The shadow emerging from the closet was all too real.

A long-buried nightmare come back to life.

Randall Gage's expression was something between a smile and a frown. "It's been a long time, Penny."

Her blood turned to ice, the shock hitting her with the force of a physical blow. She wanted to shout, to shriek at the murderer standing right before her eyes. Instead her voice came out hardly above a squeak. "Don't touch me."

Randall twirled a length of rope in his hands. His thick hair was disheveled, graying clumps standing up in spiky disarray. He was much thinner than she'd pictured, gaunt, and his cheekbones protruded from sallow skin. The green eyes burned as brightly as they had the day he'd shot her parents. Pure fright almost rendered her unable to move. Oddly, he smiled.

Her nerves shrilled an alarm. *Get out. However you can.*

She lunged for the bedroom door. Randall got there first, knocking her to the floor with a fist to her shoulder.

He slammed the door and slid the bolt home—the bolt her brother had installed as an extra precaution.

On her back, she crab-walked away, scrambling upright, almost tumbling when her legs butted up against the bed. She should scream and try to alert a neighbor, but she could hardly force her lungs to breathe, let alone yell. Terror rippled through her in torrents that prickled her body in gooseflesh. She was too scared to think. Randall Gage could not be here, in her home, in her bedroom. It had to be another horrible dream.

Randall stared at her, head cocked slightly. "You turned into a pretty lady. You still have some freckles like you did when you were a kid. Same red hair. Looks nice with your brown eyes."

"What do you want? Why did you come here?"

He appeared not to hear the questions. "Penelope McGregor, desk-and-records clerk at the fancy new Brooklyn K-9 Unit."

He shook his head. He was still smiling. "And you never even thanked me."

Her heart was thundering so loudly she wondered if she had heard him right. "What are you talking about?"

"I gave you a chance at a great life. You're a success now. Got yourself a respectable job..." He scanned the tidy bedroom. "And a nice place to live in a good neighborhood. I gave you all that." His reptilian gaze slid back to her. "You owe me, but lately I'm not sure about your loyalty."

She could only stare at him.

He frowned. "Your parents were terrible. They didn't care about you. Left you and your brother in dirty clothes, without regular meals, and they forgot about you at day care. Who forgets about their own *child*?" He shook his head. "I never would." He sighed. "They didn't love you, Penny."

They didn't love you. The very thought that was at the core of her deepest insecurity. *They didn't love you because you weren't lovable.* She clamped her jaw together as he continued.

"They were bad people. We were planning to rob the deli and they got cold feet. Did you know they intended to tip the police off and pin the blame on me? Scum, you see? No loyalty, no concern for others." He looked at her closer and his brow furrowed. "Or maybe you didn't know that. That's why you said what you did to the reporters. You didn't understand what I saved you and your brother from." He smiled, relaxing. "That's it. Don't know why I didn't think of it before."

What she'd said to the reporters? What was he talking about?

"My parents didn't deserve to be murdered," she blurted.

His jaw clenched. "Yes, they did. They were ruining your life and your brother's. They cost me everything, and they're gonna cost me my freedom, too."

She scooted a step back toward the window. If she could bang on it…

"Close it," he said.

"I…"

Now his voice was an angry bark. "I said close it. And lock it for good measure."

He came closer, so close she could smell cigarettes on his breath. She spiraled back to the bloody day when her world had spun out of control like a runaway carousel. Her parents lying murdered… Randall in his awful clown mask… The glittering green of his eyes staring at her.

"I won't."

"Cooperate and maybe I'll let you and your brother live."

He was lying, had to be, but all she could do was buy time. With shaking hands she slid the window closed and locked it.

"Even my own kin's against me now. My cousin, the hotshot US Marshal, got my DNA." Randall started to pace. "He invited me to a diner, and I got wise and bolted, but I figure he got my prints or DNA from my water glass, so now they got me dead to rights for the murders. It's been on the news. I'm a wanted fugitive, and it's only a matter of time before they get me."

She couldn't tear her gaze from the rope as he twirled it around. "So what are you doing here then?" she whispered. "Why did you come back?"

His eyes narrowed to slits, and he thrust a crumpled newspaper forward so it was inches from her face. "Because you told them I was a monster."

Ah, now she knew what he'd been talking about. She remembered the reporter on the phone, pressing her, grilling her, demanding she provide her thoughts on Randall Gage in light of the probable copycat murder that was dominating the headlines. "He's a monster," she'd said, before slamming down the phone.

Randall was watching her closely. "I know it was a misquote. These reporters are always lying to juice up their headlines. Tell me you didn't say that, Penny."

She should lie, placate him, anything to buy time, but her self-control disintegrated against the onslaught of her fear and long pent-up rage.

"I did say it," she shouted. "I said it because it's true. You are a monster." Tears she hadn't felt coming rolled down her face. "You shot my parents in the back, and you took away my childhood and my brother's. You're not some sort of hero, you're a murderer and you belong in prison."

She heard his sharp intake of breath and she knew she'd made a grave mistake by telling the truth. His nostrils quivered. A vein in his temple jumped.

"So it's true then."

Her legs trembled. Was there something she could grab to fight him off? But her fastidiously uncluttered room offered nothing she could use to save herself. There was only a neat side table with her tattered Bible, next to a bed with a teddy-bear pillow given to her by her brother on her sixteenth birthday.

Randall stepped forward with the rope, mouth caught in a grimace. Moisture gleamed in his eyes. “After everything I did for you, you turn out to be a backstabbing double-crosser just like your parents. I’m going to kill you and your brother, like I should have done all those years ago.”

“No,” she said, forcing out the word. “You’re going to prison. Like you said, it’s just a matter of time. They know it was you, and they’re closing in.”

A slow, thin-lipped smile formed. There was no warmth in it, no humor—only the promise of death. “Then I’m going to make sure you both die before they put me away.”

She screamed and lunged again for the door, but he loomed over her, holding the rope and reaching for her throat.

TWO

As he pulled up to the curb in front of Penny's Sheepshead Bay home, Detective Tyler Walker marveled at his partner's—Dusty's—unflagging energy. The golden retriever had been through a strenuous training session the day before to keep her tracking skills in good shape, and still she was looking at him in hopes that there would be a game of fetch in the offing. Humans should have such energy.

He could sure use a dose, more so now that his thirty-second birthday was looming ever closer. Why did ear infections suddenly strike his eighteen-month-old daughter, Rain, in the wee hours? The answer didn't matter. Four hours in a Brooklyn emergency room until the doc stuck an otoscope in her ear and prescribed a course of antibiotics. Feeling the usual stab of single-parent guilt, he'd kissed her sleeping cheek and tucked her into the cot in his mother's apartment, tiptoeing out to head to the station at 5:00 a.m.

Yawning, his mind returned to the question that had plagued him for six months. Was the killer clown who'd orphaned Penny and Bradley McGregor also responsible for the death of four-year-old Lucy Emery's parents? Or was it a copycat killer using the clown-mask MO? The Emerys had been killed on the twentieth anniversary of the McGregor murders, which provided juicy fodder for the media. Randall Gage or a copycat? The copycat notion was favored by the cops.

Lucy was just too young to provide the police with much to go on. Tyler and Dusty had been beating the bushes trying to locate Lucy's "friend," some brown-haired guy named Andy, who might be a key witness. Recently, out of nowhere, the little girl had said she missed "Andy." But no one knew to whom she was referring. So far all Tyler had accomplished was to waste countless hours.

He got out and knocked on Penny's door, which was decorated with a wreath of fall leaves. Didn't surprise him. Penny was the one who made sure the fall decorations were up at the office and the "pumpkin spice" creamer was stocked in the fridge. The quiet redhead was relentlessly cheerful, and her optimism mystified him. She, above all people, had every reason to be hardened toward the world.

While he waited, he chucked a ball for Dusty. It rolled behind a garden pot bristling with rosemary. He knocked again and checked his watch. Five minutes past her typical time. Unusual for the rigidly prompt woman. He texted her and waited for a reply, but he got none.

A wisp of tension rolled through his stomach. He eyed the adjoined property. All quiet with the neighbors. He gently tried the handle. Securely locked, just as it should be. She might have taken a phone call. The cop on patrol had reported an all-clear from his earlier drive-by. Dusty had finally got the ball and pranced into her spot at his side as he headed down the alley between Penny's place and the next building. Overhead, a leaf-filled gutter dripped. A drop of cold trickled down the side of his neck. He wiped it away.

Dusty brushed against his leg. *Work time?* she seemed to say.

"Just a routine check," he told her. He left the typical parade of cars and dog walkers behind as he plunged deeper into the alley. Side door secure. One frosted bathroom window, high up, small, was closed tight, as far as he could tell.

That left the rear corner.

Penny's bedroom window faced the alley. It wasn't a scenic view, but you took what you got in Brooklyn. He'd listened to Bradley tell his sister in no uncertain terms to keep her window closed and locked, and the curtains drawn. The autumn glow trickled between the buildings, dazzling his eyes as it reflected off the white paint. Shading his brow with one hand, he looked again. And then he heard it, the faintest muted scream. Alarm bells clanged in his mind, and he grabbed his gun and let himself into the gated backyard.

He tried the window and found it locked. He could not see anything through the drawn curtains. The screams continued, curdling his blood as he radioed. "Requesting backup at the McGregor house." He raced to the patio and grabbed a heavy metal chair.

"Stay," he told Dusty. The dog whined but obeyed, plopping down on the grass. Dusty was a tracking officer, not equipped to attack, and wasn't wearing body armor—he would not put his partner in harm's way.

He lifted the chair, adrenaline pumping. No time for stealth. With all his strength, he heaved the chair into the window, praying it would not hurt Penny in the process. Then he swung it in a wild spiral to break out the remaining glass. He gripped his gun and darted a quick look over the ruined windowsill. Randall stood facing the window, holding a rope around Penny's throat. Penelope's fingers clawed at Randall's as she struggled to breathe.

"Police. Let her go, Randall," Tyler shouted. He took aim, but he could not risk hitting Penny. Randall walked backward toward the bedroom door, dragging Penelope with him. When he reached the threshold, he threw her down and sprinted into the hallway. Penny fell to her knees, gasping. Tyler vaulted through the broken window.

He radioed an update and dropped to his knees next to Penny. He had one eye on the open door, his gun still in his hand. "It's okay, Penny. Try to breathe slow and easy." Settling her on the floor with her back against the bed, he raced to the front window in time to see Randall disappearing through the gate, headed for the alley. The rope he'd used to choke Penny was on the entry tile floor. Everything in him wanted to run after Randall and chase him down like the useless vermin he was. Right now, though, his task was to keep her safe until help arrived in case Randall tried to circle back to finish what he'd started. Gritting his teeth, he sent another radio update and a request for an ambulance. Then he turned back for Penny. She'd drawn up her knees, and was hugging them with her arms. Every part of her was trembling violently.

"An ambulance is coming." He eyed the red marks on her throat and rage prickled through his body. "Can you talk?"

She didn't answer.

He cupped her chin in his hand and gently tipped her face to his. "Are you hurt anywhere besides your throat?"

Finally she shook her head. "He was going to strangle me." She blinked, gulped. The whispered words held more terror than he'd thought possible. It infuriated him. No one should be able to terrorize anyone else, especially a decent person like Penny McGregor.

"We'll get him."

She didn't answer. Why should she believe him? Randall Gage had remained at large for twenty years. Even her adoptive father, Terry Brady, the lead detective on the case back then, hadn't been able to flush out the McGregor killer in spite of his dogged commitment. But now the cops knew exactly who the killer clown was, and the net was tightening. They would capture Randall Gage, no matter what it took. He squeezed her arm when a precinct cop arrived, hand on his gun.

Tyler filled him in. "I'll be back as soon as I can. Ambulance is rolling." As much as he wanted to stay with Penny, he couldn't take another moment to soothe her. Randall Gage might be slipping out of their grasp with each tick of the clock.

He hustled into the hall. Calling to Dusty, he let her sniff the rope before he jogged out the front door and charged into the alley. Dusty immediately put her nose to the ground and zoomed along, confirming for Tyler that Randall had indeed come this way. He might be able to fool his human pursuers, but he could not escape Dusty's relentless nose. No one could.

The alley was silent, a tidy corridor between the McGregor backyard and the set of nearby shared houses. It was empty save for a bike chained to a water pipe and three garbage cans hugging one wall. There was no other cover here. If Randall was hiding behind the cans, Tyler would just have to hope he wasn't armed.

He gripped the gun. This time, Randall wasn't going to get away. He was going to pay for what he'd done to Penny, Bradley and their family all those years ago. If he'd killed the Emerys, he'd pay for their murders, too.

Showtime.

* * *

Penny sat huddled on the small throw rug, shivering. *This is what shock must feel like.* The terror was so close to the surface it had sent her nerves into a kind of spastic pattern. A stupor took over her body, interrupted every few moments by a spasming of her muscles as her mind flashed through the details.

Randall Gage. His image was distorted and grotesque, like a fun-house mirror. She'd dreamed so often about his return and now that it had happened, she felt only gnawing disbelief. But this really was her home, and she truly was huddled into a ball on the little hook rug she'd made. Her neck ached where the rope had bitten into her skin.

It was a mistake to let you live.

You first, then your brother.

She tried to breathe slowly through her mouth to quell the rising panic. *I'm not a victim*, she repeated, but now the words rang false. Randall Gage was back, and he would have killed her if Tyler hadn't intervened. Maybe she really was a helpless child again, her life in the hands of the same horrible clown. Her throat throbbed and she fingered the abrasion as the fright bubbled anew.

"Penny," a voice thundered from the hallway.

"It's my brother," she told the cop.

Bradley pushed through, his Belgian Malinois, King, shoving in beside him, ears erect and nose quivering. He put the dog in a sit and crouched to hug her. His grip was so tight it almost hurt as he peered into her face.

"Are you injured?"

She shook her head. "Not badly."

He scanned the marks on her neck, his expression darkening to fury. "I heard the call and turned around. It was Randall? Positive?"

She nodded, gulping down a breath.

His grip on her forearms tightened. She

saw her own tortured expression mirrored in his brown irises.

"He's angry that I called him a monster to the press. He—he believes we should be grateful to him for killing Mom and Dad."

Bradley jerked, his mouth flattening into a hard line. "This is going to end," he insisted and she could see the pulse throbbing in his throat. "He's not going to hurt you again."

His radio chattered. As much as she wanted to be consoled, to hug her brother tight, she knew the passing moments were crucial.

"Tyler went after him."

Bradley got up, squeezing Penny's hand one more time as another uniformed NYPD officer appeared in the doorway. She was followed a moment later by Sgt. Gavin Sutherland. He immediately took a knee next to Penelope, brow furrowed. "You okay, Penny?"

She forced her head to nod up and down at her boss, but she didn't think it was very convincing since her whole body still quivered with fear.

"You're safe now," he said. "Just try and keep breathing slowly, okay?"

She complied as best she could.

He maintained his reassuring touch. "The house is secure. Ambulance will be here in a minute."

She shook her head, mortified that the sergeant, a man she respected and admired, would see her in a puddle on the floor. "I don't need an ambulance."

"Her throat…" Bradley protested. "He tried to strangle her."

"It's okay," she said, barely managing to get out the words. "Tyler interrupted him before… I mean…"

"I'm going to back up Tyler," Bradley growled as he released King from the sit. The dog gave off as much energy as Bradley, pulling at the leash to speed their departure. King, like his master, lived to chase.

Gavin shot Bradley a look. "We have a team in place. Leave it to them."

Bradley's eyes blazed. "Is that an order? Are you commanding me to lay off pursuit of the man who killed my parents and almost murdered my sister?"

Gavin squeezed Penny's arm and rose to his feet. "No," he said calmly. "I won't make that an order…at this time, but Tyler's the lead on this so you'll follow his direction." There was a touch of steel in his voice.

Bradley jerked his chin and blew out a breath. "Fair enough. Thanks, Sarge."

Penny could keep the panic inside no longer. "You should stay here. Randall said he's going to kill us both. Let the other cops track him." The words seemed to hang in the air. Bradley cast one glance at her. His expression was caught somewhere between ferocity and love.

"I'll stay with her," Gavin said quietly.

Bradley turned and ran out, King right behind him.

Penelope wanted to scream at him to come back. What if Randall killed him?

Her only blood family, the person who had been her rock since she was old enough to remember?

Gavin spoke again to the other cops before he returned his attention to Penelope. “It’s okay. We’ve got a dozen of New York’s finest out there, including Tyler and your brother. They’ll get him.”

She could not answer through the crush of fear. All she could do was follow his advice and force her lungs to keep working.

“Front is secure, Sarge,” said another officer from the doorway. “The house next door is unoccupied, family away on vacation. There’s an elderly neighbor on the other side and we’ve got an officer with her. We’ve alerted Detective Walker. He radioed he’s in pursuit via the alley.”

Pursuit. She gulped. *Please, Lord, let them be safe.*

Sarge nodded. “Get the crime-scene team in here.” He turned back to Penny. “Do you think you can stand?”

"Yes. I'm really not hurt," she said, trying to sound confident.

He grinned. "That's what your brother said after he got hit by a cab running down a purse snatcher. Must be a family trait. I'd like to have a medic check you out, anyway. You can wait in my vehicle."

Somehow she rose to her feet, leaning on Sarge's comforting arm. With every step her fear increased.

What if Randall Gage was lying in wait for Tyler and Bradley?

Tyler heard someone behind him. He jerked a look. At the mouth of the alley, Bradley and King were beginning their approach. He gestured for the pair to circle the block and cut off Randall's escape at the other end. They about-faced and disappeared. He followed up with a radio message. With dozens of cops, armed and amped to capture Randall Gage, communication was crucial.

Though he strained to listen, he caught

nothing but the sound of the wind and the typical hum of Brooklyn traffic.

Tyler put Dusty in a stay and crept forward, weapon drawn. Inch by inch he got closer to the trash cans until he'd drawn alongside them. The metal sides were dappled with moisture and rust. He held his breath against the feral stink. An image of Rain flickered in his heart, tiny, so full of wonder at the world, so completely vulnerable and perplexing. She was his heartbeat, twined into the fabric of his soul, and he prayed God would give him another day to be her daddy. Right now, duty came before daddy—it was the most difficult part about wearing a badge.

One slow breath to clear his mind, and a count of three. He plunged around the cans, nerves firing on all cylinders, weapon cocked.

No one.

Breathing hard, he scanned past the garbage cans, spending only one more moment wondering before he called to Dusty.

The retriever leaped up, nose glued to the ground as she raced over.

"Track," he said, needlessly.

The vomeronasal organ in the roof of her mouth allowed her to "taste" certain smells. It took her less than fifteen seconds to solve the mystery. Pressed right up to a low basement window, she sat, bottom waggling. He surmised the window had been left unsecured by the vacationing family and Randall had used it to his advantage.

"Good girl, Dusty," he whispered. "We'll have playtime in a minute."

He radioed the update, and the first-in NYPD commander made a plan to seal off the perimeter. Tyler jogged with Dusty to take up a position at the rear of the house while a team alerted SWAT and prepared to make entry in the front. In spite of the cool temperatures, Tyler was sweating. Dusty barked as they approached the back corner of the house.

Tyler's mind raced. There was no way

Randall could sneak through this police net. Not this time.

As he cleared the corner, some deep-down instinct screamed at him, but he did not have time to deflect the blow as Randall Gage swung a baseball bat at his head.

Penny didn't even remember the ride to the hospital. Her only thought had been that Tyler was hurt—to what degree she did not know. The waiting room was crowded with cops and dogs. Everyone was on pins and needles waiting for the doctor's prognosis.

Bradley leaned against the wall, King at his side. The anger blazed off him like a beacon, so different than his normal easygoing demeanor. He hadn't needed to tell her Randall had escaped the police net. That was clear from the barely contained rage emanating from him and all the officers gathered around waiting for word about Tyler. More trickled in with each passing moment. Raymond Morrow with his springer spaniel, Abby, and Noelle Orton whose accomplished yellow Lab, Liberty, was under threat from a drug smuggler who had a bounty on the dog's head. The team was a solid family, even though they were newly established. Her heart swelled at the thought.

Penny touched the abrasions on her throat, which had been pronounced minor. Bradley insisted on her being examined by a doctor, and she hadn't had the strength to argue. When Bradley's jaw was set, there was no use trying to change his mind.

Detective Nate Slater was engaged in an intense conversation with Sarge, who held Dusty's leash. The dog twitched forlorn eyebrows, watching every new arrival eagerly for signs that someone would take him to Tyler. Murphy, Nate's yellow Lab, was sprawled nearby in sharp contrast to Bradley's Malinois, King, who appeared as agitated as Bradley. Her brother bobbed his knee so violently that Penny wanted to shout at him to stop.

The digital clock read a few minutes after 10:00 a.m. No coffee, she thought with a start. She usually went into work early to be sure the coffee was properly prepared for the officers along with a plate of snacks on Wednesdays, if she'd had time to bake. It was her small way of helping them over the Wednesday hump. But she had not made it to the office, not today.

Don't be silly. The Brooklyn K-9 officers and staff were fully capable of providing for themselves, but it pained her that she'd not performed her self-appointed duty. The simple routine soothed her, reminded her that the world was still turning and she had a place in it. "You had a good reason to miss work," she whispered to herself.

Fear pricked her skin again at the memory of Randall's green eyes, the clench of his calloused hands on the rope he'd looped around her neck. Any moment she felt she might wake up from a nightmare and find out none of it was real.

"He could be coming after Lucy again, too," Nate said.

Nate had even more motivation to see Randall caught than the other officers. He and his new wife, Willow, had adopted the orphaned Emery child.

Lucy, Penny thought with a shiver, the little chubby-cheeked innocent. If Randall really was the one who'd executed Penny's parents, not a copycat killer, would Lucy be in danger again, too? Then an image of another girl popped into her mind—petite, wild-haired Rain, Tyler's daughter.

That stopped Penny's thoughts cold. Penny was fine, Lucy was fine. Tyler was the one in the hospital bed, unable to go home to his toddler.

She knew all the cops in that waiting room were praying right along with her that Detective Tyler Walker would be okay. "Lord, please—" It was all she got out before the doctor shuffled in.

THREE

Everyone bolted to their feet, even the dogs, as the doctor approached.

"Detective Walker is going to be fine," she said, removing her green paper cap. The group all seemed to exhale at once.

Penny's knees almost buckled in relief.

The doctor continued. "The blow hit at an awkward angle instead of a direct impact to the temple, which would probably have killed him. He's escaped a serious concussion. We'll keep him for observation today and if his morning exam goes well tomorrow, we'll release him."

Gavin nodded. "Best news I've heard all day. Can I talk to him?"

She jotted something on a clipboard before nodding. "Yes, briefly. And he's asked to see Penelope and Dusty. I can show you to his room."

Gavin laughed as Dusty surged from the floor and yanked at the leash. "I think Dusty already knows where her partner is." He spoke to his officers, directing one to provide a ride to the hospital for Tyler's mother and Rain and dispersing the others back to their duties. "I will let you know if I find out anything helpful." He turned to Bradley.

"You'll wait here for Penny, I assume?"

"You assumed right. We have to discuss safety measures we're going to put in place." He narrowed his eyes. "And this time she's not going to argue."

Meekly, Penny followed Sarge down the hall to Tyler's room.

Entering the tiny hospital room, her stomach jumped. It was so strange to see the strong and competent Tyler Walker prostrate and swaddled in a clean white sheet. His right temple was bruised, the eye blackened and puffy.

Dusty immediately got up on hind legs, front paws on the mattress, and began to lick whatever parts she could reach on her partner.

Tyler laughed and scratched his dog behind the ears. "I'm all right but couldn't you have warned me about the baseball bat?"

Gavin shrugged. "She probably tried to, but you were going pedal to the metal."

Tyler finally quieted the dog and glanced at Penny. "Are you okay?"

She blushed, hot to the roots of her hair. It was the curse of the ginger, the flush that stained her face at the slightest discomfort. "Yes. Perfectly fine. The doctor says you'll be okay, too," she said brightly.

"Yep," Gavin said, "and he'll have a restful couple of days while he's off duty recovering."

Tyler frowned. "No way."

Gavin straightened. "It's protocol. Don't fight me."

"Randall is close. You need every cop on this."

"We're covering all the major transportation systems and bringing on extra cops for overtime. If he's out there, we'll get him." He raised a palm as Tyler struggled up higher on the bed. "Two days. You can spend your off time with your daughter."

His eyes blazed azure fire. "What about protection for Penny?"

"Bradley and I are working that out. I'll take Dusty with me. You're here until tomorrow and back on duty Friday, if the doctor approves. Copy that order, Detective?"

Tyler opened his mouth, then closed it. "Yes, sir." He heaved a sigh that seemed to come from his toes. "What am I supposed to do lying here in a hospital bed?"

Gavin offered a cheerful smile. "I'm sure there are some great cooking shows on TV you could watch. Your culinary skills are deplorable. We're all still recovering from the meal you provided at the last potluck. What was that called?"

"Spaghetti Surprise," Tyler said glumly. "It was a surprise, all right."

Penny hid a smile as Tyler grimaced.

Gavin looked at his phone. "I'll check in with you soon. By the way, your mom and daughter should be here within the hour."

Tyler shot Gavin a dark look as he exited.

An awkward quiet unrolled between them. Penny pulled in a bolstering breath. "Umm, I am sorry. That you got hurt, I mean. I should have tried harder to get away." Her pulse went all skittery, the way it usually did when she tried to talk to Tyler.

"I was doing my job, that's all. Not your fault." He went silent.

She felt her flush deepen. Had she said something wrong? Again? "Well, anyway, if there's anything I can do..."

"There is, as a matter of fact."

She brightened. A task was just what she needed. "What?"

"Can you please keep Rain from seeing me like this?" His blue eyes were pleading. "I know my mom is going to charge in with tears flowing, and I don't want my daughter to be part of that." He paused. "I was hurt once before, clipped by a car when Rain was an infant. My wife, she's my ex now, freaked out when she saw me in the hospital all banged up. She almost dropped the baby. Understandable, I guess. She was young, like you."

Penny felt the sting of that statement. She was young, but capable and mature. Wasn't she? It wasn't the time to try and change his perception. "I'd be happy to watch Rain while your mother visits," she said. "I'll just wait to intercept her in the hallway."

"Cops there? You shouldn't be alone."

"My brother is lurking with King."

"Don't go anywhere by yourself. It's too dangerous."

She tipped her head to one side and fixed him with a look. “You don’t have to tell me that, Tyler,” she said quietly. “I know better than anyone what Randall Gage is capable of.”

Two spots of color rose on his face. “I apologize. I didn’t mean to talk to you like—”

“Like I am a child?”

He sighed. “Yeah. Real sorry. Sometimes I lack tact, to put it mildly.”

“It’s okay. I’ll go look out for your daughter.”

“I appreciate it.”

A moment or two of babysitting wasn’t much to offer, considering the detective could have been killed trying to run down Randall. She let herself into the hallway. At least it was one small thing and perhaps Tyler might begin to see that she wasn’t a helpless child herself if she could take care of his daughter.

Helpless child.

The flashback exploded in her skull—

her parents lying on the floor, so terribly still. And she'd stood there completely vulnerable while Randall pressed a toy into her hand.

For twenty years she'd worked hard to convince herself she was not helpless, like she'd been at four years old, but now a deep well of uncertainty had opened up again inside, black and cold.

A warm palm stroked her forearm and she snapped out of her reverie.

"Lost in your thoughts?" Bradley said.

More like drowning in her nightmares. She didn't bother to force a smile like she would have with the rest of the world. Bradley would know. He always knew.

"I am telling myself that you all are going to catch Randall before he hurts anyone else."

"We are." Bradley's tone was clipped. "And while we're working on that, Eden Chang is hopefully going to extract the evidence to determine whether or not he's responsible for the Emery killings also. He'll go to prison for life."

Instead of comfort at his words, she felt the prickle of a panic attack starting up in her stomach. Randall was still at large. He'd promised to kill. Would they find him in time? Teeth set, she did a quick round of controlled breathing. *Lord, help me to be strong*, she silently prayed.

Because deep down she knew the nightmare was beginning all over again.

It took a good half hour for Tyler to calm his agitated mother. Francine Walker was a high-strung woman. It probably hadn't helped that her younger son had decided to enter into a dangerous profession after her older committed to a life in the military. She'd been a widow for two years, since Tyler's father died of a heart attack. She watched Rain for him faithfully and never wanted to take a day off from her babysitting duties, even when he practically strong armed her.

"Mom, I don't need anything, really."

She glanced around the hospital room and poured him water, anyway.

The concept of relaxation was completely lost on her, and unless she was performing some kind of service, she wasn't content. One time he'd paid for a weekend stay at a charming Brooklyn bed-and-breakfast for her birthday. She'd returned in a cab within three hours of her departure.

"I am sorry, Ty," she'd said. "I just can't lie there in a feather bed when I know you and Rain need help."

After straightening the tissue box and refilling his water pitcher, she shoved her silver chop of hair behind her ears and pushed her glasses up her nose. "Are you sure you don't want me to bring in Rain? She's just outside in the hall," she said, fretting. "It will help cheer you up to see her."

Nothing would help cheer him up except Randall behind bars. His head ached and his lower back twinged. “No,” he said firmly. “She shouldn’t see her daddy with all these hospital trappings and his face all banged up. I don’t want her scared. I’ll be home tomorrow.” He softened his tone. “Thanks for coming, Mom. I don’t know what I’d do without you.”

Tyler wasn’t sure his father ever did love him or want him, but God had blessed him abundantly in the mother department.

She squeezed his fingers. “If only I’d been able to talk you into being an insurance agent or something.”

He smiled. “I worked in an office for four interminable months before I went to the academy, you will remember. Believe me, everyone was happy I decided to pick another career. They told me I scared the clients.”

“That’s because you glower when you’re irritated.” Her tone was playful, but he could see the tightness around her mouth. He pressed a kiss to her fingers.

“I’m okay, Mom. Really.”

"It's just that I know you're not going to stop." She shoved again at her hair. "You're going to keep after this killer, aren't you?"

"I have to. He gunned down Penny's parents and maybe another little girl's, too. I have to get this guy off the streets."

She sighed and moved away. "Since I would be wasting my time trying to cajole you into another career choice, I'm going to go talk to the doctor. Make sure he ran enough tests."

"The doctor is a woman, and she's done MRIs and X-rays of every square inch of my brain, what there is of it."

"Well, I'll just stop at the nurse's station and ask if we can have a nice chat, your doctor and me. She can tell me all about how to take care of you after you get sprung from here."

Before he could stop her, she'd scooted out of the room. As the door slowly closed, Tyler caught sight of Penny sitting with

Rain in a chair. He heard a few bars of high-pitched singing.

Gingerly he got out of the bed and opened it a crack, comforted by the sight of Bradley and King standing close. Bradley was absorbed in a phone conversation, but his eyes didn't miss a thing. He winked at Tyler and continued talking.

Penny's long red hair was down, mingling with his daughter's fine blond curls that defied any type of containment. She had Rain facing away from her, guiding her chubby hands to clap the rhythm to some song about wheels and buses. Rain's grin was toothy and wide.

His heart lurched. An innocent passerby might have mistaken Penny for Rain's mother.

But Rain's real mother, Diane, had decided before her baby was even born that she didn't want to be a parent, not then, not to his child.

I made a mistake. I wasn't ready for

marriage and I'm certainly not ready to have a baby.

They'd talked, fought, cried and talked some more, but Diane didn't love him or the baby growing inside her enough to stay. Diane was emotional, volatile, restless, a rolling stone—all the things Tyler wasn't. Those differences had been fascinating to them both at first. Gradually, he'd come to accept that he wasn't what she wanted, but he could never understand how Rain wasn't. His Rain, his beautiful daughter with the dazzling grin and the naughty disobedient streak that exasperated him, was worth dying for.

In the back of his mind, he'd been so sure Diane would have a change of heart when she held their baby for the first time. She hadn't, and he'd become mother and father to a squalling newborn who cried more than she was ever quiet.

Mostly he figured he was doing a pretty decent job of it, but often at 3:00 a.m. he would wake up worrying about all the mysterious things he didn't understand about women. Why did they cry when they were happy? How come they marched into the restroom in groups instead of alone? How could they be so incredibly strong and tender at the same time?

And most of all, how would he ever manage to teach Rain how to be a woman when he had no clue what made them tick? So absorbed was he in his thoughts, that it took him a moment to realize Penny had noticed him.

She smiled, blushing that cotton-candy hue.

He nodded, mouthed the words *thank you* and quickly closed the door again.

The sight of Penny cradling his daughter did not leave his mind as he climbed back into bed, pain throbbing through his skull. He felt more determined than ever to catch Randall before he could harm Penny, or Lucy, or any other person ever again.

God would give him what he needed to succeed. He was sure of it.

FOUR

Penny settled into her chair behind the front desk of the Brooklyn K-9 Unit on Friday morning. The beautiful three-story limestone building, with its neatly arranged work spaces, soothed her. Officers milled in and out on official tasks or guided their dogs to the training building next door, which also housed the kennel runs. The scent of her personally ground coffee mix perfumed the air.

She typed with machine-like precision, ruthlessly determined to keep her mind off what had happened two days ago. No, she would not be taking any more time off, she'd told her boss, Gavin "Sarge" Sutherland. Work was what she needed, what she craved. Trying for some sort of normalcy, she'd gotten up early, baked a pan of soft ginger cookies and ridden with Bradley into the office. It had been a long, quiet drive. Though she'd heard Tyler Walker was still off duty, she wondered what she would say to the serious cop when he returned. It had never seemed as though he had much interest in talking to her. What, after all, did they have in common? He was a cop, a single father, and she was a twenty-four-year-old desk clerk without even a niece or nephew to care for. What's more, he probably came from a normal, two-parent family, unlike her dysfunctional situation, scarred by violence. No wonder they had so little to talk about.

Gavin called to her from an open doorway. "Penny, would you come here a minute? There's someone I want you to meet."

To meet? Puzzled, she made her way to the conference room, where her boss stood, bending to scratch a fawn-colored dog with two enormous ears that flopped over at the tips. The dog immediately scuttled over and sat at her feet, tail thumping.

"Well, look at you," she said, kneeling to stroke his head. The dog whined, crowding closer, and she cupped his muzzle between her hands. His eyes were riveted on hers as though she was the only person on the planet.

"This is Scrappy," Gavin said. "He's some sort of German-shepherd mix, though we haven't done any DNA testing to see what the other part is. We found him scrounging for food, no collar, tags or microchip. You could practically see right through him he was so skinny."

An orphan, Penny thought, massaging the dog's ears until his eyes rolled in pleasure. A soft whine escaped him.

Sarge chuckled. "We thought he'd make a great K-9 cop, but he promptly flunked out of the Queens training program because he has a bit of a focusing issue." He sighed. "He just flunked out of a service-dog program, too, so it seems he's not cut out for public service. Since he gets along okay with King, I suggested to Bradley that maybe he'd be helpful to have around. Maybe, you know...a good companion."

Penny jerked a look at Sarge. "You brought him here for me?"

He nodded. "I will warn you he's prone to misbehaving. I had him in my office just long enough for him to devour the bologna sandwich I had on my desk. Incredible the way he opened the plastic bag and snatched the contents like a first-class thief. I also have yet to replace the pile of chewed-up pencils he left for me. Now that you've been told about his criminal tendencies, do you think you're up to the task?"

"I have no idea," she said. "I've never owned a dog before." She remembered as a child being completely infatuated with her daycare provider's terrier named Mr. Bigsley, who would be brought to the facility on special occasions. Mr. Bigsley had played with her sometimes, when she was the only one left waiting for pickup. He seemed to be watching over her. A shudder started up in her spine when she considered that Randall had been watching, too. And he'd almost killed Tyler Walker while trying to get to her.

Scrappy blew a breath through his nostrils and pressed his face into her stomach while she massaged his neck. Such trust, she thought. Incredible how dogs could decide in a blink to whom they would hand over their hearts.

"I'm just not sure I'd be very good at owning a dog."

Gavin considered for a moment. "He really needs someone to be his whole world, Penny."

His whole world? Tears pricked her eyelids. How could she be that when her own world had just fractured into millions of sharp-edged pieces? Randall was back, and her universe had been shaken so badly she could hardly string two words together, let alone take on a naughty dog.

But Scrappy wiggled his behind and kept his warm wedge of a head pressed close to her as if to say, *I am here to love you.*

To love you.

"I—I guess I could give it a try," she said.

Sarge smiled. "I was hoping you'd say that."

She closed her eyes to stave off the tears. On her knees, she circled her arms around Scrappy's sturdy neck and buried her nose in his fur. Too overwhelmed to speak, she hugged the dog and cried. Scrappy sat quietly and offered a gentle lick to her cheek. Instantly she knew she'd met the best friend she'd ever have.

With a soft click, Gavin gently closed the conference-room door and left her to share the moment with Scrappy. She suspected her boss felt sorry for her, and it made her cringe. She'd fought so long and hard to shed her "victim" identity. But in spite of the tidal wave of fear that threatened to overwhelm her, somehow she knew that this exuberant creature would remind her that she would never be alone as long as he was alive. Resolutely, she wiped her face and collected her wits. Scrappy wagged his tail in encouragement.

She got up and reached for the jar of dog treats in the cupboard, kept there in case a K-9 meeting went on a bit too long.

Scrappy watched her intently. "Okay, Scrappy. First lesson. Sit." She said it with conviction, like she'd heard the cops do.

Scrappy immediately rolled over onto his back, legs paddling in the air. She laughed. "That's not a sit."

Scrappy looked so cute, she gave him the treat, anyway. He hopped to his feet and gobbled the biscuit. "We'll work on that."

Scrappy's whole being broadcast such enthusiasm that she gave him another rubdown.

"Well, Scrappy, if we're going to be best

buddies, this office is going to become your second home. Let's go get you settled in. I think I know where there's an extra cushion if you're not too picky." He scrambled alongside her, nose quivering.

She hoped the presence of her new dog wouldn't make her even more of a spectacle among her coworkers. Bad enough that there was now a brigade of officers constantly checking the house she shared with Bradley and plans afoot for an officer to bunk there whenever her brother was away. An alarm system was being installed that very afternoon under her brother's watchful eye. They arrived at the check-in area after she retrieved the spare dog bed.

"This is my desk, Scrappy. What do you think?" She placed the dog cushion in a quiet spot next to the water cooler.

Scrappy sniffed around for a moment. He trotted to his cushion and dragged it into the leg space below her desk, circled three times and apparently found the accommodations suitable.

She gaped. "Well, where are my feet supposed to go?"

He answered with a tail wag.

Laughing, she sat in her chair and tucked her toes under the edge of his cushion. Comforted by his solid furry weight draped across her feet, she breathed in the pleasure of her neatly ordered work space. Stapler, just so, neatly framed picture of her and Bradley at his badge pinning and a lush indoor plant that Bradley had dubbed "Frondy." Now that she had Scrappy for a desk mate, everything felt perfect.

The second pot of coffee was perking in the kitchen. The next shift of officers beelined straight for the coffee and creamers and helped themselves to her platter of cookies. She felt the knot of tension loosen ever so slightly as her routine duties absorbed her mental energy. Scrappy kept watch, ears swiveling, when he wasn't snoring softly.

During her morning break, she even dove cautiously again into plans for the October open house, mulling over details as she let Scrappy have some exercise and a few treats. She'd decided there would be a pumpkin-decorating area as well as a craft table set up for the children.

"We'll need the fat color crayons for the younger ones," she murmured as she scribbled a note to herself back at her desk. It was Rain she was thinking of. The feel of her small hands in Penny's, her high-pitched laughter, had awakened something unexpected. She'd never allowed herself to think of having her own children. That was far too idyllic a picture for a woman whose own parents had neglected and often forgotten about their children. With her lifelong struggles against insecurity and fear, she knew she was not proper mother material, but for some reason it was extremely satisfying to tend to Rain.

FBI Agent Caleb Black startled her from her thoughts. She jerked. A long-time member of the search team hunting Randall, Caleb held up a napkin-wrapped treat. "Sorry. I just wanted to thank you for the cookies. I came by to touch base with Gavin, and man was I happy to see your home-baked goodies." He grinned. "Your treats are the best perk of having a temporary desk in this office."

"You're welcome. I…" Her voice trailed off as Tyler strolled through the door in jeans and a long-sleeved navy T-shirt. His temple sported a purplish bruise, but he looked much less haggard than before as he stood across the front counter from her.

Caleb quirked a grin. "What part of 'off duty' did you not grasp?"

"I'm not on duty. I was just in the neighborhood and I wanted to run something by you about Andy."

Penelope knew that Tyler and Bradley

had been working overtime chasing down a lead provided by young Lucy Emery, who'd shared that she missed her friend Andy. The elusive Andy might just be the witness who could provide information about whether or not Randall Gage had killed the Emerys.

Caleb cut off her thoughts. "And I thought you just came in because Penny baked your favorite cookies."

Tyler inhaled deeply, eyes closed for a moment. For a quick moment, his face softened and he appeared younger. "Ah. That is the smell of those ginger cookies, isn't it? The ones with the sugar crystals on top?"

"Yes, those are the ones." Penny hadn't realized the cookies she'd chosen to bake were Tyler's favorites. Or had she remembered that, deep down? Was he lingering in her subconscious mind, too? She hadn't been able to stop thinking about him lying in that hospital bed. His battered face emerged in her mind. She fiddled with her stapler.

Tyler's gaze dropped. He let out a deep laugh, which further erased the weariness. "Easy, boy," he said to Scrappy, who had come to stand on hind legs and peer at him over the edge of the counter, ears swiveling. "I'm a dog person, truly, but Dusty is out having her nails done so you might not recognize that." Tyler stood still as Scrappy gave him an exploratory sniff and he slurped a tongue over Tyler's offered hand.

"This is my new best friend, Scrappy," she said as the shepherd mix resumed his spot at her feet. She buzzed Tyler through.

He met her eyes as he moved to her desk. "I'm glad you have a buddy." His voice went soft. "How are you doing?"

"Fine, just fine." She straightened the stapler again, feeling the rise of heat in her cheeks at his intense gaze.

Caleb finished his cookie. "I've got a few minutes to chat, Ty, but if Gavin sees you here, I'm going to say you forced me to talk to you at gunpoint. I don't want any friction between the FBI and Brooklyn K-9 Unit."

Tyler smiled. "Fair."

She noted the tension in his wide shoulders. She realized he had not, in fact, let go of anything in spite of being ordered off duty.

Caleb headed off to the conference room but Tyler lingered. She could detect the fresh smell of shampoo from his hair.

"I just, er, I mean, wanted to thank you again for helping with Rain. She's been asking about you, in fact."

Penny looked away. "No problem. Is she doing okay?"

"Yes, except for her general misbehavior. The ear infection is better, and she felt well enough to flush a box of crayons down the toilet. That's her new hobby. Flushing. The whole concept fascinates her. I think she's going to be a plumber."

Penny laughed. "I'll make a note of that

when I babysit her again." She stopped abruptly. Had she said, "when" instead of "if"? Did he think she was insinuating she wanted him to ask her? As the heat threatened to paint her face in scarlet, Tyler spoke.

"Rain and I read about a million stories yesterday when I got sprung from the hospital, after I uncorked the crayon clog, but at bedtime she wanted to sing. My rendition of Johnny Cash's top ten hits did not do the trick. You'll have to teach me that bus song sometime, the one with the wheels and stuff."

"I'd be happy to."

"Okay. Uh, everything feel secure at your place?"

"Secure as Fort Knox."

"As is should be. Precious material inside."

Precious? Her? He seemed to be startled at what he'd said. "Well, anyway, gotta go get one of those cookies before Caleb fills his pockets."

"I can always make more."

"You'll never find anyone here to try and dissuade you."

He lingered.

She shuffled papers, still feeling his presence like the warmth from a lit torch, until her cell phone pinged. As she read the text message, she knocked over her tray, showering paper clips down upon Scrappy, who yelped.

She stared at the phone, unable to pull in a full breath. Terror pulsed through every muscle and nerve as she reread the text.

I almost got you. Next time, I'll finish it.

Tyler saw Penny bolt to her feet. The rolling office chair shot backward and slammed into the water cooler. Scrappy scrambled up, whining and circling her ankles, as Tyler surged forward and took her by the shoulders. "What is it? Tell me."

Her lips moved, but no words came out. Her face was bloodless. He walked her backward and settled her into the escaped chair. Scrappy pawed at her knees.

Tyler ignored the agitated animal. “Take a deep breath.” A tremor rippled through her body as he held onto her forearms. She shuddered. Several other officers moved closer.

“Ambulance?” Officer Lani Jameson asked, worried.

“I’m not sure,” Tyler said. “Give us a minute.”

Scrappy could take it no more. He leaped into Penny’s lap and shoved his nose to her neck. Her arms encircled him, and she tipped her cheek to graze along his ears. The dog seemed to poke through Penelope’s fear, and Tyler silently thanked the funny creature.

She looked up and pressed her phone into Tyler’s hand. He read the threatening text, and his gut hardened into iron.

Randall Gage.

Anger flashed hot through his bones as he thrust the phone at Lani.

Her voice was tight as she answered. “He never gives up, does he? I’ll call Eden.”

He brought Penny a glass of water and stayed close until the tech guru was summoned. Eden Chang chewed her lip as she examined the information on Penny’s cell phone.

“It was probably sent from the dark web again, like the first couple. I’ll research it, but I doubt it’s going to lead anywhere helpful. I’m sorry.”

He’d learned that the “dark web” was a whole vast network of encrypted online content that wasn’t indexed by search engines. Basically, it was a criminal’s paradise for buying credit-card numbers, all manner of drugs, guns, counterfeit money, stolen subscription credentials and software that allowed them to break into other people’s computers.

He put a hand on Penny’s shoulder, earning an ear swivel from Scrappy. “Come sit in the break room until you feel better, okay?"

She shook her head, straightened in the chair and scooted Scrappy to the floor. "It's not time for my break yet." Her voice quivered.

"That doesn't matter. This is a unique circumstance."

Her lips pressed into a thin line. "It does matter. I'm going to stay at my desk until my break. I have a bunch of work to catch up on and the monthly reports."

"Don't be silly—" he began.

Her mahogany eyes sparkled. "I am not being silly. I am going to do my job." Each word was precise as cut glass.

That's when he realized her hands were balled into fists on her thighs and the sparkle in those luminous eyes was the precursor to tears. Why had he used the word *silly*, as if she was a child? Right now she was fighting to hold onto her independence, to preserve some shred of dignity in the face of a monster who was determined to kill her. Work was her life preserver and he'd just minimized that. *You're a real sensitive guy, Tyler.*

He stepped back a pace. "I'm sorry. I don't think you're silly. I was concerned, but I should not have said that."

She nodded, body still stiff and taut as she stood, rolled her chair back into place and sat again. Scrappy trotted cheerfully to his self-appointed spot at her feet. He licked her ankle as he set up watch. "I'll need to work on my reports now." She gulped. "Please."

The tiny stroke of desperation in that last word lanced an arrow right to his heart. He forced a smile. "Sure thing."

She began to type on her computer, slim shoulders ramrod-straight. Anyone would think she was completely composed, save for the trembling of her fingers on the keys. Caleb walked over, clipping his phone to his belt. "I've got to take care of something on another case. We'll have to talk later, Tyler."

Noelle Orton joined them, her slight form made larger by the bulletproof vest. Her yellow Lab, Liberty, flapped her ears as she approached. The dog was a beautiful specimen with a distinctive black ear marking.

"I was talking to Eden when Lani called about the text." Noelle gestured to Penny, brow wrinkled. "She okay?"

"She's putting up a pretty good front."

Caleb shook his head. "Guy murders her parents and comes after her and her brother twenty years later? I'm impressed she can even leave her house. She's got amazing courage."

Amazing courage, his mind echoed. Far beyond her years.

Gavin arrived and spoke quietly to Penny. His eyes narrowed as he caught sight of Tyler.

"Walker..."

Tyler raised his palms. "Not on duty. I promise."

Gavin sighed. "Why am I not surprised?

Meet me in my office and tell me what we have on this text."

Tyler filled in Gavin and met with Eden with no tangible result. An hour later he checked on Penny again and called Bradley to bring him up to speed. He could hear his friend's anger crackling in his tone.

"We gotta get him, Ty," Bradley almost shouted. "He's torturing my sister."

"I know. We will." Caleb approached as he ended the call.

"Bradley?"

Tyler nodded.

"How's he taking the text?"

"Let's just say his blood pressure is edging toward the roof."

"No doubt."

Caleb followed him down the hallway, and they ran into Noelle exiting her cubicle with Liberty at her side. Her expression was alive with excitement. "We got a tip on Holland."

Tyler froze. Ivan Holland was the Coney

Island drug smuggler who had put a bounty on Liberty's head for messing with his operation. The dog had almost been run over in the latest attempt, along with Noelle, who had been walking her at the time. Everybody on the team was hankering to bust Holland for targeting a member of their police family.

"According to a tipster connected to Ivan's crew, they've turned on him after he killed that informant. They don't want to be a part of his police vendetta—it's drawing too much attention. He's got no one on his side now. Tipster tells me he's been hanging around Flatbush."

"When?"

"This morning."

Tyler's stomach rolled in anticipation. "Who's talking to the locals?"

"I will," Noelle said.

"I want to be in on it, too," Tyler said.

"Nope," Noelle said. "You're not even supposed to be here."

"I'll come in an unofficial capacity. Help

you take notes." In fact, Tyler felt a burning desire to help Noelle bust Holland. It would be a big load off his plate and clear the way for him to devote most of his time to catching Randall.

Noelle arched an eyebrow.

Tyler pressed on. "I'll ride along as a civilian escort. Dusty needs an outing, especially after her grooming. She can't stand grooming days."

She was still frowning. "If Gavin finds out..."

"Tell him Tyler forced you to take him at gunpoint," Caleb said as he headed for the door. "We've already covered that."

Tyler held up his hands. "I promise. I'm riding along only. Purely a civilian thing."

Noelle laughed. "That's how you spend your day off?"

"If it gets Ivan Holland off the streets, I'll happily sacrifice. Can we stop at the training center and get Dusty?"

"No problem."

Tyler jerked a look at Penny. "I'll meet

you outside in ten, Noelle. Got to check on something."

Noelle and Liberty walked outside. Noelle's brow was furrowed, and he understood her determination. Capturing Ivan Holland was personal.

Penny was still at her desk, staring at her screen.

She gave him that cheerful smile again, but he noticed the slight pinch of her lips.

"Doing all right?"

She nodded. "Bradley is going to have my cell-phone number changed. I'll be okay now. No more texts hopefully."

If only Randall's threats could be neutralized so easily.

"Is there anything I can do? Something you need?"

She fired a bright smile. "Not a thing. I'm surrounded by cops with a guard dog on my feet. Perfectly safe."

He wanted to press further, but she was already staring at her screen, typing with amazing dexterity.

"I'll be back in a couple of hours, well before you leave. At quitting time, I'll take you home, all right?"

Her fingers paused on her keyboard. "No need. My brother will escort me."

He wondered if she was still stinging from his "silly" comment. Or was she merely hanging onto the formalities of work because it kept her from thinking about other things?

It suddenly occurred to him that he himself had come into the office, to the comfort of work and routine, when he could just as easily have accomplished his discussion with Caleb over the phone. Then he'd inserted himself into a police assignment with Noelle. So who was clinging to the comfort of a work routine now?

He cleared his throat. "You have my cellphone number, but if anything changes and your brother isn't available, call me, okay? Or, you know…if you want to talk or anything."

Pink suffused her cheeks. "Thank you. I

will call you if I need to." He saw the muscles of her throat convulse as she swallowed. "That's very kind."

Still, he could not make himself walk away. "Promise me you won't leave without me or Bradley?"

"Yes, I promise."

"All right. I'll see you later." He'd cleared the counter, willing himself not to turn and look at her again, when she spoke.

"Tyler?"

He stopped. "Yes?"

"Randall has been at large for twenty years. What…?" He heard the hesitation in her voice. "What are the chances you are going to catch him this time?"

"This time?" He locked on her soft brown gaze. There was such vulnerability there, raw emotion shimmering in her irises. "One hundred percent."

Her whispered follow-up split his gut in two.

"Before or after he kills me?"

He walked back to her desk and kneeled there, earning a nose poke in his thigh from Scrappy. Pulling her hands away from the keys, he forced her attention to his.

"Penny, we are going to put Randall away before he hurts you or anyone else again. I know it's hard to believe, but now we know his identity and we will get him soon, very soon. You just have to hold on and trust."

The brown of her irises softened to a lighter café au lait. "Honestly, I don't know if that's possible. I've not really trusted anyone but Bradley since my adoptive parents passed." She paused, her mouth pulled into a thoughtful bow. "But I will try."

Without thinking, he pressed a kiss to her hand. "I won't let you down." And then he strode out, not wanting to detect any shock in her face from his gesture that had shocked him plenty.

Kissing her hand? Promising that he

would keep Randall from ever hurting her again?

And strangest of all, feeling deep in his soul that he desperately meant to keep that promise, no matter what the cost.

FIVE

Penny walked Scrappy at lunchtime in the grassy area provided for the police K-9s. He pranced and sniffed, enjoying the cold autumn breeze. She was reassured by the constant parade of cops and dogs. They all checked on her solicitously.

She kept a smile fixed in place as she responded politely and later forced herself to eat her peanut butter sandwich in the break room. When she went to fill a glass with water, she returned to find the remainder of her sandwich gone. Scrappy swiped the crumbs from his lips with a satisfied slurp.

"You are a naughty dog, Scrappy," she scolded.

She grinned and caressed him. "How

about tomorrow I bring you a chew bone so we can have a lunch break together, okay?"

She got a tail wag of agreement. Tummy full and energy depleted, he settled under her desk for a nap while she tackled the outstanding paperwork and ordered a box of supplies for the open house. By late afternoon, she'd almost forgotten the terrible text from Randall. A glance out the window told her that evening was coming. The growing darkness sent a chill cascading down her spine. She wasn't afraid of the dark, was she? No, not the dark, just the man hiding in it.

Bradley called a little after four.

"Sis, I'm stuck on a stakeout."

Her heart began to pound.

His voice cut through her fear. "Tyler's almost there. He's bringing your phone with the new number."

She swallowed and forced a calm tone. "But he's off duty."

"He grumbled so much that Sarge said

he could take over your detail when I'm not around."

She remembered Tyler's kiss on her hand, a warm spot she imagined she could still feel. "But he's got Rain to take care of. I'm sure I could ask another officer..."

She looked up to find Tyler striding in with Dusty. He twirled a key ring around his finger. His eyes were shadowed with fatigue, she thought, or maybe frustration. The hunt for Ivan Holland had not yielded any results. Or perhaps he'd begun to regret his decision to be her babysitter.

She covered the phone. "Bradley told me you were coming, but really, it's fine. I can get..."

He shook his head, which seemed to make him wince. "No, I want you with me, but I have to pick up Rain from day care. Do you mind? I figured we can get some dinner at my apartment before your brother comes home."

He said it so matter-of-factly, but the very idea whipped up her nerves. Dinner? At his apartment? "Um, well, I've got Scrappy. Maybe I should..."

"My building has a dog run. We can stop with the dogs before it gets too dark."

Dark. Again, her stomach flipped. *Go home, lock the door and hide until morning*, her mind yelled. But she would not live that way. She'd spent too long hiding in the shadows and fought too hard to make her way out of them. She forced back her shoulders.

"Okay." She ended the conversation with Bradley and disconnected. "I'll get my purse."

Her knees only shook a tiny bit as she left the secure station and stepped into the darkness with Tyler, Scrappy and Dusty. They walked quickly to his vehicle. Tyler's sharp gaze traveled along the street and between the vehicles.

Looking for Randall, she thought with a shiver. Gratefully, she slid into Tyler's civilian vehicle, an SUV.

She watched as Tyler settled into the

driver's seat. The interior was meticulously clean except for a lone bag of fishy crackers lying on a car seat in the rear.

"Better grab that bag," she told Tyler, as Scrappy hopped in, nose quivering. "He's not very reliable around food. I found that out the hard way."

Tyler chuckled. "Neither is Dusty, but she does a great job tidying up anything Rain has dropped."

He turned on the engine and immediately a preschool counting song began to blast through the speakers. Tyler's face turned scarlet. "Oh, sorry. Uh, that's Rain's favorite at the moment. Something about turtles and goldfish."

Penny could not prevent her giggles from spilling out.

He quirked an eyebrow. "I don't think I've heard you laugh before. Not for a long time, anyway. It's nice."

Now it was her turn to blush. He paid attention to her laughter at work? He was always so focused, moving too quickly and purposefully to pay any mind to her, she'd thought.

They traveled the Belt Parkway at a snail's pace through the traffic until he pulled up to a four-story building with a yellow sign for Happy Tot Day Care stuck on one of the doors. Through the front window she could see small children climbing on a plastic play structure and playing with toy cars. High-pitched squealing floated through the air.

And in an instant, the long-ago sadness returned. A dull pain bloomed behind her ribs as her mind traveled back into the past. She recalled being the last child left at day care, her four-year-old nose pressed to the window in search of parents who had forgotten about her again. One by one the other children had been picked up until the facility went quiet. Penny had stayed among the abandoned toys, trying not to notice the lengthening shadows or the agitated pacing of the teachers. She recalled Miss Deborah's brightly painted fingernails clutched around the phone, a combination of annoyance and pity in her voice.

"How could they forget their own kid?" she'd whispered. "And they don't even wash her clothes or brush her hair. They probably don't feed her breakfast before they dump her off here, either."

It was the truth. Bradley, barely fourteen, was the one who toasted bread for her, cut it into triangles and added butter, if there was any in the fridge. He packed her after-school snack, too, a hastily assembled collection of whatever he could find instead of the neatly partitioned containers brought by the other children who shared her day care. She remembered the laughter of the other kids when she'd found half a baked potato in her bag for snack. She would have been perfectly content eating that potato, but she'd gone hungry rather than face the laughter of her peers.

Sometimes it was Bradley who'd come

to retrieve her after he returned home from a full school day and a couple of hours at his part-time job to discover her missing. She remembered those long afternoons, looking into the eager faces of the parents as they'd hugged their children and hastened them to cars, admiring their crayoned pictures.

She'd tried taping her own painstakingly drawn pictures on the front of the dented refrigerator, hoping it would help her parents think about her, remember her…want her. If the pictures were good enough… If she just tried hard enough…

She heard Randall's words again. *Your parents didn't love you.* Tyler's touch on her shoulder made her jump.

"Sorry. You looked sad there, for a moment."

She blinked. "I…spent a lot of time in day care. Randall was a handyman and he did some work at the place. That's how he met my parents. They got into some bad things, together. Planned some thefts and scams and such."

Tyler listened intently, though he was no doubt privy to all the facts, anyway. For some reason, she felt the need to say it aloud. "Randall knew… I mean, he noticed my parents, uh, forgot about me sometimes. That's part of the way he justified killing them." She gulped. "He said they were bad parents and I suppose he was right. It took me a long time to understand that it wasn't my fault that they neglected me. I always thought if I was different, more appealing somehow, prettier, smarter…"

Tyler took her hand. His fingers were long and warm as he gently squeezed. "I'm sorry. None of that should have happened to you, or any child for that matter."

She shrugged, garnering strength from his big palm. "It's okay. I have a great brother, and my parents did what they could with what they had. Plus I had two amazing adoptive parents."

He still held her hand, warming it between his. "But you still have some past scars to work through, right?"

"I know my biological parents' behavior wasn't because of me, but sometimes the feelings creep up and I have to give myself a stern talking-to. I guess with Randall coming back it's natural I'd start to stew about things again." She flashed a smile at him, but his face remained grave. She gave his hand a jaunty wiggle before she let go. "Really, it's okay."

"I wouldn't have brought you here if I had known it would be so painful."

"It isn't. I'm all right."

His face still showed uncertainty.

"Well, Detective," she said, voice bright. "Since I know you aren't about to let me stay in the car, let's go get Rain. Scrappy and Dusty can hang out now that the fish crackers have been secured."

He paused, azure eyes troubled. "If it's too hard to go in there maybe I can have someone bring her out to me. I'll just make a phone call."

Warmth tickled her tummy at his thoughtfulness. "No. It's good for me to see all the kiddos at pickup time. It reminds me how families are supposed to be, how God made them to be."

He nodded, and she wished she had not shared something so deeply personal with him. He was, after all, only babysitting her.

Gulping in a deep breath, she walked with him into the day care.

Tyler carefully placed the still soggy finger paintings in the trunk area after strapping Rain into the car seat next to the two eager dogs. The artwork was a mishmash of yellow, all yellow. The teacher had said she could not be persuaded to try any of the other colors. Funny how that small girl knew exactly what she wanted. He wished he had such clarity.

Rain delighted in the new doggy, whom

she called "Sappy." Since she insisted on her counting music, he turned up the sound and Rain and Penny sang together. He chimed in at the chorus for good measure, which earned him a brilliant smile from Penny.

That smile had to be a million watts and it left him speechless for a moment. What a splendid thing to possess so much joy when she'd endured a mountain of hardship. He resolved to try to coax a smile from her again soon.

On the drive back, he kept a wary eye out for Randall, but there was no one tracking them that he could detect. When they reached the brick apartment building, he parked and they let the dogs out for a rollick in the fenced dog run. Again, there was nobody around who shouldn't be.

He led the way to their third-floor apartment. "My mom lives downstairs," he explained in the elevator on the way up. "She joins us for dinner. Hope that's okay. I think the Friday-night dining tradition started as a way to ensure I was not poisoning her only grandchild with my cooking."

He was unlocking the door when his mother appeared in the hallway, a covered dish clutched between two pot holders. "Well, hello." Her eyes went wide as she took in Penny with the eager Scrappy at her shin. "I didn't know you had a dinner date, Ty."

Tyler grimaced as he let Rain inside. Scrappy and Dusty beelined in. "Not a date. Mom, you met Penelope McGregor at the hospital. She's Bradley's sister. You know, my buddy who manages to be over here every time you make fried chicken?"

"Of course. I always make a couple of extra pieces figuring Bradley will eat a few." He discerned a calculating look in his mother's eye that gave him pause. "So nice to see you again," she said as she walked after them and put her casserole dish on the counter. Pausing to clasp Penny's hand, she said, "You have the most lovely red hair, Penelope. Just the most attractive shade, like an autumn sunset."

Though he had a feeling his mom was about to meddle, he agreed. Her hair did remind him of a glorious sunset. He blinked.

"Thank you, and please call me Penny. But the red hair comes with a maddening amount of freckles, which got me teased plenty in school."

Rain brought Penny a stuffed rabbit. The toy's face was discolored by a set of ink eyebrows that she had drawn on after discovering a marker in Tyler's desk drawer. She bent and took it. "Who is this?"

"Babby," Rain said solemnly.

"Babby the rabbit. Shall I take care of him for a while?"

Rain nodded.

Penny cradled the bunny like a baby and Rain trotted off in search of another toy.

His mother beamed. "Rain must really like you, Penny. She doesn't hand Babby over to just anyone. Babby is her right-hand rabbit. Did you see that, Ty? Look how she's taken to Penny."

"Yes, Mom, I saw," he said. "Thanks for making the lasagna. It smells great."

"Tyler is the world's worst cook. If I left it up to him, Rain would starve or turn orange from an overdose of mac and cheese. I suppose that might be my fault since I was always the chief chef and bottle washer when my husband was alive. He always had to have things just so and I never wanted my boys to feel the pressure of trying to cater to his food whims." She paused for breath. "Do you like to cook, Penny?"

Tyler sensed again how the wind was blowing. His mother was shifting into full matchmaker mode. "Mom, would you mind setting the table while I fix a salad?"

"Oh, sorry, Ty. I can't. I have to run along."

He stared. "You're not staying for dinner?" He couldn't remember the last time they'd eaten Friday dinner without her.

"Nope. I'm so busy. I've got a zillion things to do."

Like what? he wanted to ask, but the door was already closing behind her.

Penny appeared to be trying to smother a giggle.

"My mom's not too subtle, huh?"

"I think she was hoping you had a date. I take it that's not a frequent occurrence."

He sighed and got out the salad bowl, fishing in the fridge for lettuce, tomatoes and carrots. "No. Dating is not on my agenda. I told her I have my hands full with Rain, but she won't accept that." He paused. "She feels bad. Her last matchmaking effort resulted in me marrying a woman who left two days after Rain was born, so our track record is terrible, anyway."

The giggle died away. "I'm sorry."

He shrugged. "It was a mess, of course, but I'm coming to realize that it was for the best. If Diane stuck around, she would have resented it and passed that feeling on to Rain. I wouldn't ever want Rain to feel like she was unwanted." He froze. "I… I'm sorry. I'm sure that's not how your mother felt." *Blockhead move, Ty.*

To his great relief, she smiled. "It's okay. I've had a lot of years to puzzle it out and I like to think my mom loved me the only way she could, even if it wasn't the way I wanted or needed."

He nodded. "I get it. My dad loved me, too, I suppose, but he was an unhappy guy, never satisfied with anything or anyone. Mom said she wouldn't ever hold it against him since he gave her two sons. Diane gave me Rain, so I'll always be grateful for that." A memory of Diane flicked across his senses, her blue-black hair fanning out across the hospital pillow.

Something in her expression when she'd been handed Rain after the delivery had finally hammered home the truth, even though he hadn't allowed himself to believe it then. He'd been so certain that she would react like he had. Tears had run down his face and his hands had shaken so badly he could almost not support the perfect life that had just emerged into the world. His daughter, a perfect baby, an undeniable delivery straight from God.

Diane had looked over her daughter. "She's beautiful, isn't she?" she'd asked.

He'd only been able to nod, the emotions stripping away his speech.

She's ours, he'd wanted to say until her expression stopped him.

She's yours, Diane said with her eyes.

And that's when the terrible realization began to sink in. Diane was not going to parent this baby. Further, she was not going to stay with him, either. Nothing had changed in that hospital delivery room, for her, anyway.

He found himself saying the words aloud. "I was sure Diane would fall in love with Rain once she held her, like I did. I think she was just too young to..." He trailed off.

"To be a good mother?" she finished softly.

Why was he always saying some dumb thing when he was around her? He heaved out a deep breath. "I guess that's what I told myself. The blaming hurt less than admitting she didn't love me or Rain enough to stick around. In retrospect, I wasn't the best husband. I didn't try to understand her very much and I worked around the clock."

He recalled one particularly nasty argument they'd had when she'd spent several nights in a row out with her friends. "I need a life, Tyler," she'd insisted. "My friends understand me better than you." But had he ever tried to get to know her friends? Join in their activities? He sighed.

"She said I didn't know how to have fun and maybe she was right. I know I could have tried harder."

Had he really admitted that? He'd never really formalized the thoughts until that moment, but it was true. It wasn't solely

Diane's age that killed their relationship. He could have—should have—done better.

The divorce was wrapped around with feelings of intense shame. He didn't like to think of the conversations they'd had, the way he'd pretty much begged Diane to stay. The love had died on her end long before it ebbed away for him.

"Fun looks different for different people," Penny said.

He looked for judgment in her expression, but he didn't find it there. Penny was young, too, but he could already see she had plenty of maternal instinct. It shone in her smile and the soft brown of her eyes. His heart thunked against his ribs.

"Does Diane have much contact with Rain?"

"No. She sent a card on Rain's first birthday, but other than that, she hasn't checked in once. I haven't changed my cell phone or email addresses because Rain is going to want contact with her mother at some point. Frankly, I'm dreading the day I have to explain the situation to her. How am I going to tell her that her mother didn't want her?"

"You love her. You'll help her understand it wasn't about her. Some very kind people in my life helped me to see that."

Something about her sweet smile made him want to press a kiss to her lips. He was dumbfounded by his own thoughts. Penny was a colleague, Bradley's sister, and what's more he was supposed to be keeping her safe, not admiring her character or thinking about kisses. He stood there, addled, but she'd already begun to wash the lettuce for the salad.

Grabbing some paper napkins, he slapped them on the table. While the lasagna was cooling, the three of them gathered around the coffee table to build a block tower. It didn't get very high as Rain knocked it over once with her elbow and Scrappy did the same with his tail. They settled for making a block corral for Babby to sit in.

As Penny and Rain added the finishing touches, he stood to stretch the kinks out of his back. He went to the window and gazed down at the busy street below. It was almost fully dark outside. Somewhere out there, Randall was plotting to kill. He looked back at Penny and Rain bathed in the glow of lamplight. Their giggles filled the room with sweet music that had been missing for a long time. One false move, one careless moment, and Randall would snatch her life away. Though he knew there was really no chance anyone could see into his apartment, he pulled the curtain closed, anyway.

It gave him the sensation that the three of them were cocooned in the soft light. If he could only prolong the time, keep the thought of Randall far away from this happy moment. Penny had watched him close the curtains, then quickly refocused on the blocks. Randall would never be out of Penny's thoughts until Tyler put him away forever. After that, would she be ready for marriage? Would he ever be again?

Unsettled, he went about serving up the lasagna and pouring ice water into glasses and milk into a sippy cup for Rain. The dogs had been fed and lounged nearby. He guided Penny into a seat and slid Rain's chair, with the attached booster setup, close. Babby was given an honorary seat and even his own plate and spoon for his imaginary meal.

"What is Babby going to eat?" Penny asked.

"Candy," Rain said with a maternal nod.

"Nature's perfect food," Tyler said.

Penny grinned. "Babby gets to start with dessert and skip the vegetables. That's a pretty sweet deal."

As he began to say grace, the happiness of this family scene, so long missing from his life, clogged his throat. Embarrassed, he found he could not continue.

Penny smoothly finished the grace, and Rain added her own vigorous "Amen!"

He sent her a nonverbal thank-you and she acknowledged with a quiet smile.

He found himself staring at Penny as he ate his meal. Was there really a loving, sweet red-haired beauty sitting across from him, chatting with his daughter? She seemed so interested in what he had to say, in helping Rain to manage her dinner, almost like she belonged there. The cold note of reason intruded on his happiness. She wasn't here because of him…it was merely a safe place to land until her brother came and fetched her. She was here for protection, not because she was looking to get to know him and Rain any further. He swallowed wrong and coughed into his napkin.

Keep things cordial and professional. It was sage advice, but as the evening wore on, he found himself thoroughly enjoying her company. When the meal was over, he was sorry. He firmly declined her offer to help wash dishes.

"No thanks, I got this. I happen to be

a master dishwasher even if I can't cook a lick. Rain looks like she's angling for a playmate. Feel free to defend yourself if she tries to drag you into the play area." He gestured to a corner partitioned off by a folding screen. "Don't feel obligated. I am making it my life's mission that my daughter will learn the meaning of the word *no*."

Penny laughed. "I'm sure a bit of play-time with me won't upset your entire disciplinary agenda."

Penny and Rain trundled off to the play area with the two dogs. Soon he heard Rain snap on her kiddie music player and the clamor of cheerful music started up. While he washed and dried the dishes, his mind drifted back to Randall, who was even now making plans to murder the gentle woman who was playing dress-up with his daughter. He smacked a plate into the dishwasher harder than he'd meant.

Not gonna happen.

Bradley tapped on his door as he was drying off the counter. Tyler let him in.

Bradley inhaled with a look of rapture. "Man, it smells good in here."

Tyler laughed. "No thanks to me. It's my mom's lasagna."

"I figured you didn't make it if it smells this great."

"I will pretend I didn't hear that. Have some." He cut a square, plated it and handed it over along with a fork.

Bradley ate a massive bite and rolled his eyes. "Excellent. Where's Penny?"

He pointed to the corner. Another song about ducks and frogs began. "It doubles as the playroom."

Bradley nodded as he chewed, keeping his voice low. "Penny's a natural with children. I tell her that, but…" He stopped.

"But?"

"She's just not sure of herself. Thinks she wouldn't be a good mom because of our own parents. Scared it's in the DNA or something." He shrugged. "Never mind.

I shouldn't be talking about her business. Thanks for pitching in while I was tied up."

"No problem. Happy to help." He would not tell Bradley exactly how happy he felt at having his sister around. "What did you find out today?"

He forked in another mouthful. "Nothing about Randall, but I talked to Lani on my way here. That guy Joel Carey says he's got a photo that will prove Brooke and her pups are his."

Ownership of the gorgeous stray German shepherd and her pups had been a source of controversy since they'd been rescued from an abandoned building site. The pups had become a favorite of everyone in the department. Brooke, the mama dog, and her clan had been getting meticulous care at the police veterinary center. The whole unit had fallen in love with the adorable, precocious puppies. Tyler had even taken Rain to see them.

Joel Carey insisted he was their rightful

owner. He was mistrusted by all the cops, including Tyler. Carey's timing was suspicious since he came forward right after a heartwarming news piece aired featuring the dogs. The dog was named Rory, he claimed, and she'd run away when a fire broke out at his place. The fire had conveniently destroyed all of Carey's ownership records about the striking animal.

"I still don't buy it," Tyler said. "Carey's just looking to breed or sell them to make some money. We can't just hand them over."

"If Carey produces a photo of himself with Brooke, we're not gonna have much choice." Bradley wolfed down another bite of cheesy noodles. "Tell your mom I'm going to name my firstborn after her."

"That will be dicey if you have to call your son Francine."

"Good point. I'll hope for girls. What'd you and Noelle find on Ivan Holland?"

"Nothing concrete, but we're getting closer. He's in the area and he's getting desperate as his people turn on him. Matter of time." He waited until Bradley swallowed and addressed the elephant in the room. "Eden is working on the text he sent Penny, but..."

Bradley's eyes darkened. His tone hardened, like it had when Tyler had called to fill him in on the newest threatening text. "But she's going to get nothing, just like the last time."

"Randall might be playing with you and Penny. Maybe he's moved out of the area. It would be smart after what he pulled at your house. Could be he's just bluffing about trying again."

Bradley set down the plate a tad too hard. "You and I both know he's not going to stop. Getting her a new phone number is like putting a bandage on an arterial bleed. Have we got extra eyes on Lucy Emery, in case Randall is the one who took out her family, too?"

"Nate's arranged that with Sarge." He paused. "What does your gut say, Bradley? Do you think Randall also killed the Emerys?"

"I don't know, but that's secondary at the moment. We have to get our hands on him. Now."

Tyler nodded. "Copy that."

Bradley followed him to the play corner. Tyler's breath caught. Penny sat on the beanbag chair, Rain curled up in her lap. Penelope's arms were around Rain. Both were sound asleep. Dusty and Scrappy snored away, as well, sprawled on the throw rug. Scrappy's paws were thrust up in the air. He was dressed in a pink tutu. Dusty snored away, wearing a pair of Rain's dress-up butterfly wings.

Bradley chuckled. "You'd never catch King wearing dress-up clothes."

But Tyler had eyes only for Penny and Rain.

Emotion unfurled deep inside him, like a plant blooming after a long-awaited rain shower. His daughter and Penny were joined together, as if they were meant to be that way. But surely not. She was a deeply wounded woman, determined to hold together the unraveling strands of her life. And he was an older, world-weary single father, lacking the courage to risk his heart to make another family.

He took a picture with his phone of the two sleeping on the beanbag.

Bradley sighed. "All four of them sound asleep. Too bad I have to take Penny home."

Too bad, he agreed.

SIX

Penny slept fitfully, slogging through the Saturday morning chores at their Sheepshead Bay home. She missed seeing Tyler and Dusty in the backyard, but they were back at work. *It's Bradley's turn to babysit me*, she thought glumly. At least she required less supervision than Scrappy, who had already unspooled an entire roll of toilet paper all over the bathroom and down the hall. His irrepressible curiosity reminded her of Rain. A flush crept up her cheeks when she remembered how she'd fallen asleep in Tyler's apartment, right there on the beanbag with his daughter.

Way to show him you're a competent adult. She'd been awakened by her brother's gentle patting on her shoulder, and

Tyler had then rolled Rain into his arms and carried his daughter to her bedroom. Why couldn't she have stayed awake a bit longer?

Still, the evening had been cozy and perfect, a shared meal and interesting conversation. Astonishing, how relaxed she'd felt. How long had it been since she'd enjoyed the company of a man to that degree? She did not date often, and when she did, she inevitably found a reason to break it off when the prickly panic began to creep in, the low whispers that told her she was not ready to let things progress any deeper. Marriage and family were not in her immediate future.

The squawk of a bird flying over the yard made her start. Did she even have a future anymore? With a killer waiting for his chance?

She slapped a slice of bread into the toaster to distract herself from the unsettling musings and poured a cup of kibble into Scrappy's bowl. "You are supposed to eat kibble, not peanut-butter sandwiches or toilet paper." He stared at her fixedly, but when nothing more enticing was added to the mix, he set about gobbling it up.

The house phone rang, a telemarketer she figured, but it kept right on ringing until she finally picked up the call.

"Penelope?" The quivering voice made her press the receiver closer.

"Mrs. Lawson? Is that you?"

"Yes, honey."

Penny lost the next few words until her neighbor got to "…flooding." The word was followed by sniffling. The elderly lady in the brownstone next door was a widow who rarely ventured out unless it was to deliver a loaf of her freshly baked cinnamon bread to Penny and Bradley. Widowed five years prior, she was a virtual hermit. Penny's heart sped up at the anxiety in Mrs. Lawson's voice. "You've got a flood, Mrs. Lawson?"

Bradley entered the kitchen, attention

diverted from the coffee machine by her phone conversation. King regarded Scrappy with a watchful eye. He was tolerant of the mutt, but not completely accepting yet. Scrappy was smart enough not to challenge King in any way. She put the call on speaker so Bradley could hear.

"I was just drawing a bath in the tub to soak my feet in some Epsom salt, but the faucet handle snapped off and I can't shut off the water. I tried to pull out the plug, but I can't reach down that far without falling."

The sniffling grew more pronounced.

"On my way," Bradley said.

"I'm so sorry, Mrs. Lawson. My brother will come right over, okay? He's a whiz at fixing things. It will be all right, don't you worry."

Bradley fetched his toolbox, strode to the door and disabled the alarm.

"Stay here," he said to Penny. "Bolt the door behind me."

"I will." She dutifully turned the lock after he left.

Ten seconds later, the phone rang once more.

"I'm so sorry to call again," Mrs. Lawson said, her voice quavering. Penny had to press the phone closer to her ear as the woman continued. "But can you bring a tarp? I want to protect the legs of my oak dresser. The water is flooding the tub and soaking the carpet." Penny could hear Mrs. Lawson's quiet sobbing.

"Yes, of course. Be careful not to slip, okay?" She peered out their living-room window. "Bradley is on his way up the stairs right now, I can see him at your door. I'll get that tarp." She wasn't about to disobey Bradley's direct order, but she figured it wouldn't hurt to fetch the tarp from the cellar and text him. He could return and snag it after he'd turned off the water.

King would not follow her down into the basement. He was staring out the window, tracking his partner's every move. She knew Scrappy would be at her heels all the way down the steep, narrow stairs, so she let him out into the backyard. He shot outside, rump wiggling at the thought of a romp in the yard. She locked the sliding door before pulling her sweater more tightly around herself, then went to the cellar steps and flipped on the light. The cold interior smelled of mold and old cardboard. The darkness seemed to penetrate her body. Goose bumps rippled her arms as she peered down the staircase. For a moment she froze on the threshold, breathing hard.

Thoughts of Randall and his hideous clown mask stabbed at her. *Next time, I'll finish it.* Her feet froze.

There was nothing in that basement that could hurt her. At the bottom of the stairs, she strode purposefully to the neat shelves, where Bradley had a stack of tarps. She grabbed one and tucked it under her arm. The tension inside her turned to satisfaction. At least she could accomplish one small thing without turning into a quivering lump. She would put the tarp by the front door so Bradley could easily grab it.

She'd just reached out for the railing to start upstairs, when hands jerked her backward.

She wanted to claw the fingers away, but her arms were twisted behind her back and someone pushed her hard, her cheek hitting the clammy cement wall. She sucked in a breath to scream when her captor pressed a strip of duct tape across her mouth, sealing in her fear.

"Surprise," Randall said into her ear. "Did you think I forgot about you, Penny? Did all your cop friends convince you I couldn't get close again?"

His breath smelled of coffee and cigarettes. Disbelief filled her body even as she wriggled to get loose. How had Randall done it? Probably by intimidating Mrs. Lawson. Randall had obviously threatened her into making the initial call.

Then he waited until Bradley was safely away from the house and forced her to phone again the second time, requesting the tarp.

As if Randall read her mind, he chuckled. "I saw your brother carrying the tarp through the cellar doors the last time I was watching your yard, checking things out until I was sure which window was yours. Neat trick, asking the neighbor call you to fetch it. The old lady was tougher than I thought. I had to hurt her a little bit to get her to cooperate."

Hurt her? The sweet and vulnerable widow? Terror and outrage sparked through her entire body. Her screams were caught inside her taped mouth.

"We'd better go before dear brother Bradley comes back." He leaned so close his lips brushed her ear. Disgust nearly gagged her. "I'm going to save him for a later date."

There was another rip of tape and her hands were fastened behind her back.

Then she was being marched, stumbling, toward the doors that exited to the outside. Randall forced her through and outside. He didn't bother closing up. Instead he propelled her into the alley, where a small car was parked. As soon as she saw the car, her fear bucked even higher.

Her brother's words echoed in her mind. *Never let an abductor take you to a secondary location.* She knew with sick certainty that once Randall forced her into that car and sped away, she had no hope of saving herself. Pressing her heels into the asphalt, she resisted with all her might. Her shoes juddered over the rough surface. Randall stopped, but only long enough to change his grip. He turned her around, pressed his arm into her stomach and flipped her over his shoulder. Leverage gone, she thrashed wildly, trying to knock him over, or slow him down—anything to prevent her abduction. He merely grabbed her tighter and sped up his pace. Her silent screams abraded her throat.

Bradley must have surely known by now. He'd have found Mrs. Lawson and gotten the truth from her. He and King would come charging down the alley any moment. She just had to hold on for a few more seconds. With a sudden violent contortion, she tumbled free of Randall's grip.

Her knees struck the ground, causing a sharp jolt of pain. She ignored it, surging to her feet. All she had to do was get away for a split second. Legs churning, she could not maintain her balance with her hands trapped behind her back. A stumble slowed her. Randall dove at her, knocking her flat. The breath was pressed from her lungs as he pulled her to her feet and once again flopped her over his shoulder.

Her vision blurred as she was bounced against Randall. The black fabric of his windbreaker scraped against her cheek.

Stall! Fight as hard as you can for a few more seconds...

Blood pounded in her head and beat behind her temples. She kicked and bucked as if an electric current was passing through her body, but Randall was strong and determined, and this time he wasn't going to relax his hold.

Unable to scream, born along like a leaf in the current, she heard the pop of a latch.

No. This couldn't be happening. Bradley would see. Someone would come. Terror flooded her nervous system as she realized what was taking place. She was dropped into the gaping trunk of Randall's car right on top of a leering rubber clown mask.

The last thing she saw was Randall's crooked smile as he slammed the lid closed, leaving her in darkness.

Tyler smiled at Dusty in the back seat of his police car. She was curled up next to the soft pink sweater Penny had left at their apartment. Memories from their evening refused to leave his mind for very long. The dogs had seemed to enjoy their gathering as much as the humans. The two animals had tirelessly retrieved the toys Rain flung at them. He suspected both dogs had been tossed an ample supply of peas from Rain's plate when he'd taken his eyes off her. Penny might have noticed but she wouldn't rat out Rain to him.

He'd enjoyed the evening probably much more than he should have. It had been a very long time since he'd laughed so heartily and shared so much. For some reason, she hadn't seemed upset by his talk of his broken marriage. There was something about her that calmed him, soothed a part that had been broken when Diane left. With Penny, there was safety in letting down his guard, showing his silly side. And when he saw her with Rain asleep, as if they belonged together… He shifted on the seat. He had enough to think about right now trying to find the elusive Andy and tracking down Randall. Not to mention the case on Ivan Holland, which could break at any minute if the local beat cops spotted him.

There were way too many balls in the air to be preoccupied with thoughts of Penny. Still, he found himself guiding his vehicle along the road that would take him past the McGregor home. He'd just check in with Bradley, make sure the protection schedule was complete, he told himself.

Dusty flapped her ears. "Yeah, I know we already worked out the schedule, but it couldn't hurt to double-check." Dusty blinked. Why did he feel like the dog could see right through him?

Why am I making excuses to see her outside of work hours?

He hadn't the faintest idea. Teeth gritted, he pulled to a stop a block before her home and let out a deep breath. Quickly he looked again at the picture on his phone of Penny and Rain sleeping soundly. Again, a sense of peace washed over him when he viewed the picture for the dozenth time.

He should turn around before he made

an idiot of himself. He'd flipped on his turn signal when the call came in over the radio.

Abduction.

McGregor home.

A BOLO issued for a dark-colored sedan.

Penny.

Adrenaline swamped him as he turned on his lights and siren, then punched the accelerator. He screeched up to the curb. Bradley and King were sprinting from the alley, racing toward Bradley's car.

Tyler rolled down the window and shouted. Bradley froze, then turned and hurried to Tyler's car. His face was white and pinched. "Randall took her. I saw him getting into the driver's seat. Exited the alley westbound." Bradley swallowed. "I think he put her in the trunk."

Tyler fought to pull in a breath.

Lani braked to a stop behind them, red lights flashing. "I was a block away, taking a report. What happened?"

Bradley pointed to the neighboring house. “Elderly lady named Anita Lawson was threatened by Randall into setting us up. She’s not hurt badly, but she needs care. And Scrappy’s in the yard. I can hear him barking.”

“On it,” Lani said.

Bradley had already gotten King into the car when the second report came over the radio. A patrol officer from the 61st Precinct had possibly spotted the sedan speeding on the Belt Parkway.

Tyler listened, his heart slamming into his ribs. His spirit plummeted when the cop informed them he had lost his quarry in the long pocket of residential homes and shops sandwiched between the Belt and Emmons Avenue. Randall had headed into a sleepy Sheepshead Bay waterfront community close to the marina. With multiple units responding from different directions, they’d close in quickly and cut off his escape from Brooklyn. They’d locate the vehicle and make the bust. If he headed for the piers themselves between Ocean Avenue and East 26th Street, they could cut him off there, too.

His throat went dry as he finished the thought.

But would Randall kill Penny first?

SEVEN

In the cramped trunk, the darkness stabbed through her like an ice pick. Alone. She was completely alone, like she had been on the night she watched her parents die. Randall had left her then with a deep well of uncertainty that she should do something, anything. But four-year-old Penelope had not had the faintest clue what action she should take. The phone in their cramped unit had been disconnected for nonpayment, so she could not have called anyone even if she'd thought of it. So she'd huddled into a ball on the sofa, clutching the plastic-wrapped monkey, too afraid to look closer at what was lying on that worn kitchen linoleum. The fear had taken root deep in her soul. She'd been very hungry, she remembered. Stomach growling, shaking and alone, she'd waited for her brother.

Alone. Twenty-four-year-old Penelope fought hard against the buzz of panic that electrified her. Panic was not an option, and Randall hadn't won yet. She ordered herself to calm her breathing. It was a Herculean feat since her mouth was taped shut and her body was being jostled with the car's movement. The trunk interior smelled of gasoline and rust. The flabby rubber of the clown mask pressed into her back, where her shirt had ridden up. That horrible clown face, as if it had leaped from her nightmares into real life.

She would not cry. She was not a child and certainly not helpless.

Pressing her feet against the lid of the trunk, she kicked with as much violence as she could muster. Her heels thudded uselessly against the metal, sending pain through her bruised knees and shins. The trunk did not give, and the car did not slow. Where was he taking her? When would he stop?

She knew the answer to that question. *He'll stop when it's time to kill me*, she thought with a shudder.

She needed to attract attention.

Rolling onto her side, she desperately sought the soft glow where the taillights were positioned. She found one, wriggling as close as she could. If only her hands had been secured in front, she would be able to whack at the light until it popped free. Her only option was to try it with the heel of her boot.

Contorting her body drenched her in sweat. Inch by painful inch, she got her feet into position. Aiming her boot heel, she banged at the plastic. The crunch when it gave was sweeter than music. Another round of aerobics brought her face close to the empty hole. A puff of cool air bathed her. The sedan hit a bump and smashed her cheek into the frame. White-hot pain zapped at her. This time she braced her knee against the movement and peered out the hole.

Glimpses of paved road and the bumper of a car flashed by. A delicate whiff of the sea told her they must be near the marina. Faint hope stirred. The marina area was lined with piers housing recreational fishing fleets, dinner boats and, across the water, lovely houses she could never hope to afford. It was a vibrant place with seafood shacks, gift shops and bicycle rentals. Though it wasn't as bustling as it would be in the summer months, the October weather was still mild enough that there might be plenty of people still about. But at this hour? Another bumper appeared in her tiny view hole. After a moment, it vanished, turned into another lane perhaps.

What if no one notices the broken taillight? She had to try something else.

But what could she do with her hands taped behind her?

The rubber mask.

Groping and straining, she grabbed it, willing her fingers to grasp the symbol of her worst fear. She gritted her teeth. The thing that Randall used to terrify her was going to be her salvation. As she tried to turn herself into position, the car bumped and juddered, throwing her onto her belly. Was he stopping? Her time was ticking away.

Breathing hard, she jerked her body around and fed the clown mask through the hole. Maybe if she could hold it there, wave it like a signal flag, the movement might attract attention. A violent bump of the car caused her to lose her grip and the mask fell through the hole. She cried aloud.

She tried to peer out and see where it had landed, but she only succeeded in banging her face against the metal again. Gradually, an important detail eclipsed the feelings rampaging through her.

Every nerve telegraphed the dreadful message. The car was slowing. Randall was pulling over somewhere. Her plan had failed and now he was coming to kill her, just like he'd promised. She heard the engine die.

Her brother would find her. Someone surely would come.

Footsteps crunched along the side of the car. She readied her feet to kick out, to knock him backward and earn herself a few precious seconds. The plan was unlikely to succeed, but it was all she had.

Help me, she silently prayed. *Don't let him kill me.*

A key scratched in the trunk lock.

She blinked back the tears. Whatever happened, she would not give him the satisfaction of seeing her cry.

Tyler braked to a stop at the entrance to the marina parking area and slammed a hand on the steering wheel. "Where is he?" Behind him, Dusty whined.

Bradley's increasing tension crackled over the radio. "I've checked the parking lots and we have units on both ends of the street. What's your location?"

"Parking lot by the piers. Nothing so far. I..." He stopped in midsentence. "Hold on a minute." He was out of his car and sprinting to the spot where a crumpled object was lying on the asphalt. A clown mask with blue hair and a slashed mouth. Had Randall stopped and opened the trunk? Continued on, or reversed and returned to the main road? There was only one way out of the parking lot. Either Randall had escaped the lot before Tyler had shown up, or he was somewhere nearby, perhaps behind the boathouses or the warehouse at the end of the long row of boat slips that lined the Sheepshead Bay waterfront.

He almost shouted in the radio pinned to his shoulder as he broadcast the location. "I've got a clown mask. I'm going to have Dusty track."

"I'll be there in five," Bradley said. He didn't ask Tyler to wait. Tyler wouldn't have listened, anyway.

Unwilling to waste a moment lingering around for a reply, he released Dusty from his vehicle, clipped on her long lead and brought her to the mask.

"Track."

The command was unnecessary. Dusty was already nose-deep in the rubber recesses of the mask. Three long whiffs and she took off across the parking lot. He pulled his sidearm and followed.

Nose glued to the ground, she led him to the last row of cars. There at the very end was the black sedan. The rear taillight was missing. Pulse roaring, he put her in a stay and edged forward, weapon aimed at the driver's-side window. Another step closer and he darted a look into the front seat. Empty. Rear seat, also.

The trunk lid was slightly ajar. Weapon aimed, breath held, he jerked it open. Empty. A ragged breath escaped him. Tyler wasn't sure if he should be relieved or not. Penelope hadn't been left there for him to find. Did that mean Randall hadn't hurt her? Yet?

"All right, girl," he said, calling to Dusty. "Show off that champion nose, okay? Track."

She was already twitchy, nostrils vibrating as she followed the scent from the parking lot past the dock. A row of neatly painted warehouses with corrugated roofs lined the area next to the boat slips. There was no outward indication that Randall had passed this way, but Dusty had all the clues she needed. She led him right to the second warehouse, sitting obediently at the warped wooden door and beaming those soft eyes at him.

He gave Dusty a pat and whispered, "Stay. You'll get your treat soon—I promise."

As soon as he arrested Randall Gage and got Penny to safety.

Gripping his gun, he seized the door handle and counted to three.

Penny stumbled as Randall pushed her behind a stack of pallets in the old warehouse. The place smelled of oil and the far-off fragrance of the sea. She tried to stay upright but fell to her knees instead. Sharp pain cracked through her shins and she felt a trickle of warm blood ooze through her pant leg.

Her throat was dry and aching from her muted screams. She'd struggled, thrashed and gone limp, but to no avail. Not a single soul had witnessed Randall wrestle her from the trunk and march her into the empty warehouse. He'd covered her bound hands by keeping her to his side, as if they were a couple, strolling along the dock.

The skin around her mouth stung from where he'd ripped off the tape.

"It's too suspicious having you walk around with your mouth taped. If you make any noise, I will toss you in the water and hold you under until you drown." That thought made her weak. Drowning alone and helpless, sinking to the bottom of Sheepshead Bay to her silent death while Randall watched and gloated made her nauseous. Still, she would have risked shouting out, if she had seen a possible rescuer.

But there had only been a single dock-worker, who'd been too far away to hear over the wind-tumbled waves. A couple had passed by on a boat, and her pulse quickened, but they'd merely waved a friendly hello. Randall had waved in return and the couple kept on going. Her last hope had seemed to fade away in the small vessel's wake.

She'd been praying with all her being that Bradley would catch Randall's trail. But he hadn't been able to rescue her, not this time. How would he feel knowing that he'd been tricked? It would eat away at him and the thought made her angry. Bradley should not have to shoulder any more grief. "You have no right to do this."

Randall jerked as if she'd surprised him. "I have every right. Your parents messed up my life. I saved you from them and you repaid me with betrayal, just like they did. You, your brother, your parents. The whole lot of you are a bunch of snakes who deserve to die."

She glared at him. "How exactly did we mess up your life? So my parents came to their senses and changed their mind about the robbery. You could have gone ahead without them."

His face went scarlet. "I did go ahead, and because your parents tipped off the cops anonymously, I almost got arrested. I had to lay low for two days and you know what happened in that time? Huh, Penny? Do you have the slightest clue what they cost me?"

She saw the rage simmering below the surface of his irises.

"My wife left me," he snapped. "One too many times I'd let her down. She warned me the next time I didn't come home, she'd hit the road." He shook his head. "I tried to phone, but she wouldn't take my call." His voice dropped. "On her way out of town she got in a wreck.

Killed on impact." He took a knife from his pocket and pointed it at her. His fingers were gripping it so tightly, his knuckles went white. "That's on your parents. She's dead because of them."

Penny shook her head. "They didn't mean for that to happen."

"You were four years old. How could you possibly know what kind of people they were?" His eyes rounded. "I told you the truth, and you still defend them, like they were great people. It's unbelievable. They were dirty double-crossers who never cared for you. I saved you from that, and what did you do? You double-crossed me, too. Told the world I was a monster."

She pressed down the words bubbling up in her throat. Confrontation wasn't going to get her out of the situation. Instead she forced a conciliatory tone. "I'm sorry about your wife. That must have hurt you very much. I can understand why you feel angry."

"You understand?" For a moment, she

thought she detected a softening in his face, but then he tipped his head back and laughed. "You looked just like your mother for a minute. She thought she could sweet-talk me, too." He bent close to her, the knife now inches from her cheek. "Know what that got her?"

Penny swallowed. She did know. It had earned her mother an execution. For the first time, Penny admired her parents for standing up to Randall the best way they could, for trying to make a better choice for themselves and maybe for her and Bradley. They'd failed as parents, but at the end it was possible they'd attempted to change. She longed to tell Bradley about her epiphany. Would she live long enough to share her thoughts? Her only option was to stall for as long as she possibly could.

"Why did you kill the Emerys? What did they do to you, Randall?"

He shook his head. "Not that again. Stop talking."

"Are you having trouble justifying why

you orphaned Lucy Emery? Did you think you were saving her, too, by murdering her parents?"

He edged the knife closer. "I told you to stop talking. You're giving me a headache."

But talking was the only thing keeping her alive. "You don't have to kill me. I understand now why you're so angry. I didn't know about your wife, but now that you've explained it, I'll talk to the press and tell them your side of the story. They won't think you're a monster anymore after I tell them the truth."

Slowly, he shook his head, then grimaced. "It's too late. It's a matter of time before I'm sent to prison. You and your brother are the last two items on my to-do list. Or should I say, my to-die list?" He laughed again.

So much for the soft approach. Randall was obsessed with his mission. There was no point in pretending she understood his evil. She shrugged. "So you're just a coward, aren't you? It doesn't take a big man to shoot two unarmed people and kill a woman with her hands tied behind her back."

He glared at her. "Like you said, I'm not a man, I'm a monster."

She stumbled back several steps as he advanced.

He snapped his head to one side. "Did you hear something?"

She could only detect the harsh sound of her own breathing until somewhere in the back of the warehouse a door slammed open. Her pulse thundered.

"Police!" a familiar voice shouted. Randall swung around.

Penny didn't wait. She darted into the shadows of the warehouse, almost falling over a low pile of rope. Catching herself in time, she raced down a row of shelves.

Randall was right behind her. "I'll kill you," he shouted. "It won't do you any good to run."

But she'd recognized the voice of the police officer who'd slammed through the door.

Tyler Walker was here, for her.

And she was going to do everything she could to keep herself alive long enough to make it to him.

EIGHT

Protocol dictated that Tyler should wait for backup, but that wasn't going to happen, not with Penny's life on the line. "Randall, it's all over," he hollered. A clatter from deeper in the warehouse indicated Randall, or perhaps Penny, was on the run.

He took cover behind three enormous fuel barrels and shouted again over his thundering adrenaline. "There's no way out of here. Give it up and let her go."

There was a crash from somewhere to his left. Tyler surged forward, sheltering himself next to an upside-down boat with a freshly painted bottom. He waited, straining to hear. The tiniest squeak—the sound of a rubber sole on the cement floor—alerted him. Randall must be at his three o'clock, moving quickly.

Tyler erupted from behind the boat. Past a pile of netting, he saw a flash of black. He pursued, skirting a rusted engine and a crate full of batteries. Motion ahead. Sprinting forward, he rounded a boat in the process of being refinished and stopped short.

Ten feet away he caught sight of Penny. She was half crouched, hemmed in a corner by piles of neatly stacked lumber. Her body was rigid with fear, and awkward posture indicated her hands were probably bound behind her. She snapped a look at Tyler.

He saw her mouth open as if she was about to shout to him, but a rustle from behind a pile of sailcloth snatched his attention. He aimed his weapon.

"Nowhere to go, Randall. Let me see your hands," he shouted.

Randall catapulted from behind the sailcloth. He sprinted toward Penny, his arm raised, gripping a knife.

"Stop," Tyler shouted as Randall charged. Penny screamed, twisting her body away. She created just enough of a gap between them. Tyler fired. Randall grunted, dropped the knife and clutched his side. A bloom of red appeared through the fabric of his shirt.

"Stay where you are," Tyler roared, but Randall ducked behind a row of shelving. Penny stood, eyes enormous with shock. Her gaze darted between Tyler and the spot where Randall had been a moment before.

He kept his voice quiet but commanding. "Penny, it's okay. Come toward me."

She walked as if she was on a pitching ship, each footfall a little unsteady. Everything in him wanted to crush her to his chest, but the situation was far from secure. He kept his weapon trained in case Randall appeared and tried to attack her again. When she got close enough, he took her wrist and guided her behind him toward the exit door, still searching for Randall. He felt her shudders go right through him. What could he say to comfort her? It was only by God's grace that he had gotten to her in time. But if he could take down Randall, right here, right now, it would finally be over. Freedom for Penny and Bradley.

Another cop was already through the door. Tyler handed Penny into his care. "Get her out of here."

The officer quickly escorted Penny away. Tyler could have called in Dusty to track, but as he edged around the shelves, he saw the trail of blood. As silently as he could, he whispered an update into his radio and crept forward. Following the droplets led him to a tiny office, the door ajar.

From far away outside, he heard the sound of barking, low and intense, but not Dusty… It was Bradley's dog, King. He eased open the door with his boot. A puff of sea breeze on his face sent his nerves skittering. He darted through the door. The office was small, a desk and a file cabinet jammed tight. Papers littered the floor. A small window above the desk had been slid open. A bloody handprint on the sill showed him Randall's escape route.

Smothering his frustration, he reversed course, radioing again as he went. He burst back outside, into a maelstrom of noise and activity. Penny was safe, he noted, sitting in the back of a squad car and guarded by two officers.

In the opposite direction, down by the water, Bradley was holding onto King as a cop tended to someone on the ground. *Yes, we got him*, Tyler silently crowed with satisfaction as Dusty joined him. They jogged to the dock. The closer they got, the more his instincts blared at him. Something wasn't right. His spirits sank as they neared. The prostrate figure wasn't Randall. It was a skinny young man, no more than a teen probably, dressed in jeans and a flannel shirt. An officer pressed a cloth to the man's bicep. Blood stained through the compress.

"The guy came out of nowhere and demanded my boat," the young man said, a look of outrage on his face. "I told him no way, and he cut me. Can you believe that?"

Boat? Tyler groaned as he saw the tiny motorboat growing smaller and smaller as it plowed through the choppy waves of the bay. He felt like shouting. This could not be happening. Randall could not be slipping out of their grasp again.

"Already called it in," Bradley grunted. Anger flamed in his eyes. "But he'll probably ditch the boat as soon as he can. Harbor Patrol is deploying and a chopper's en route."

Like Bradley had already noted, Randall would no doubt dump the boat within minutes to avoid being spotted from the air, so they were back to a ground pursuit. This time, they had an advantage, he thought grimly. "He's wounded. I shot him. There's a blood trail. I'll inform all the local clinics. He won't get far bleeding like that. He'll have to stop somewhere for medical attention."

Bradley's nod was curt as he locked gazes with Tyler. They both knew how close Randall had come to keeping his murderous promise to kill Penny. They made their way back to her. She bolted from the car when she saw Bradley and locked him in a tight hug. Then she wrapped Tyler in a similar embrace.

He clasped her tightly, feeling her tears on his neck, the wild beating of his heart, or was it hers? He could not tell. There were so many emotions tumbling through him he did not trust himself to speak.

"You're okay," she mumbled. "He didn't hurt either of you." She sounded as if she was trying to reassure herself.

"We're fine." Tyler moved her back into the car and eased her onto the seat again. Her cheek was bruised, blood trickled from the corner of her brow. The knee of her pants was torn and bloody. "Tell me how you're doing."

She turned a stricken face to both of them. "I'm—I'm okay, I think. Is Mrs. Lawson all right? Randall said he hurt her."

Tyler nodded. "Lani said she's very upset, but fine otherwise."

Penny bit her lip and looked at her brother. "I'm sorry, Bradley," she said, tears caught on her lashes. "I thought it would be okay to get the tarp from the basement. I should have suspected…"

"None of this is your fault," Bradley said savagely. Tyler nodded in agreement.

"As a matter of fact, you showed some real smart thinking, kicking out the taillight and shoving the mask through." Tyler was going for encouragement, but his cheerful tone rang false even to his own ears. He was still reeling at what could have happened. Randall with the knife ready to plunge into her heart.

A look of utter defeat stole over her face. "I guess if I was real smart, I wouldn't have let him get to me in the first place." Her voice wobbled and she wrapped her arms around herself.

Bradley moved away to get King settled as another wave of cops arrived. Tyler knelt next to her.

"That's on us, Penny. We should have moved you to a safe house before this, insisted on it."

"But I don't want to..." She trailed off, defeat clouding her features. "You're right. It's the prudent thing to do." Her chocolate gaze met his. "But I can still work, right? My job...it's everything to me."

He heard in her question a mountain of desperation, the passionate need to hold the threads of her life together. Reaching out, he gently touched the soft skin of her forearm. If he'd been a moment later... Cold slithered along his spine. The best course of action was to settle her in a safe house, keep here there, and avoid the office since Randall knew all about her job. He looked up to find Gavin standing nearby. He must have heard Penny's question, because he gave Tyler a slight nod.

Tyler looked at Penny again, closely this time, past the fright. He realized at that moment that Penelope McGregor was, quite simply, beautiful. Not in the common way of television models and movie stars, but in the earnest curve of her mouth, the delicate sprinkle of freckles, the way her eyes shimmered with an intensity that made his breath hitch just a little. He swallowed the feelings and took her hand.

"If you want to work, we'll talk to Gavin and make that happen for you."

She sagged a bit, her fingers ice-cold in his. "Thank you."

He paused, weighing his words as he considered what she'd been through. Locked in a trunk, bound and helpless, almost murdered. *Lord, help me to be delicate here.* "There are people connected to the department, really good doctors I mean, who can help you…process what you've just experienced. They specialize in trauma."

"I know all about doctors who specialize in trauma, Tyler." She looked away from him for a long moment before she turned back. "They can't help me feel safe again. I will never feel safe again until Randall is caught."

He fought the growing desire to tear the city apart brick by brick until he got his hands on Randall. "You are a strong person, there's no question about it, but if you change your mind, all you have to do is say the word. I'll take you myself and—and I'll stay with you through it, if that would help. You wouldn't be alone unless you wanted to be."

For a moment, she was silent, clenching his fingers. She brought his hand to her face and rested her cheek against their twined fingers. He held his breath, hoping she would feel his determination, the tide of emotion that welled up inside, the ferocious need to protect, the fear at what might happen if he failed.

And there was something more. It was as if she touched some soft spot inside him, opened a vault down deep in a place he'd kept locked in shadow since Diane had left. He pressed his mouth to her knuckles and kissed her. "I am so sorry this happened."

After a final squeeze, he let go of her hand and stood, breaking the connection between them as a medic arrived.

It was a connection he could not afford. Not now, not ever.

The safe house was not actually house, but a second-floor room in a boxy six-story redbrick hotel in Bay Ridge. Penny tried hard to banish the feelings of defeat as she surveyed her new residence. Bradley, of course, had wanted to stay here with her, but it would be foolhardy to place both targets in the same spot. To make matters worse, she was not convinced her stubborn brother was safe at their home, even with his devoted police dog, but there was no changing his mind about leaving. She wondered if he was secretly hoping Randall would show up again. The thought chilled her.

The hotel decor reflected a depressing beige color palette. One corner hosted a minifridge, a microwave and tiny coffeepot. The two double beds filled the rest of the space—one for Penny and the other for Brooklyn K-9 officer Vivienne Armstrong. Her border collie, Hank, slept on dog bed in the corner. Hank had better manners than Penny's exuberant companion. Scrappy wasted no time in jumping up on the bed as if testing the waters.

"Same rules here as home, Scrappy," she said, ordering him off the bed and onto a squishy dog cushion Tyler had brought from her house.

Vivienne looked around. "Not exactly the Ritz, but we'll make do, won't we?"

Penny gave her a bright smile. She knew Vivienne would probably rather be anywhere but a cramped hotel room, so Penny wanted to be as amiable a roommate as possible. "It will be just fine. I appreciate you staying with me."

Vivienne lifted a shoulder. "Happy to do it."

Penny endured a very long Sunday filled with cooking-channel shows, reading time and taking Scrappy and Hank out for supervised outdoor time. She sadly missed going to church, but she did some Bible reading on her own.

When things got particularly dull, she spent time peeking through a crack in the curtain at the crawling traffic below. Tyler called regularly to check in, but he did not ask to speak to her directly. The night passed in an agitated haze. Her sleep was peppered with snippets of terrifying memories. Once she awoke panting and crying, fearful that she'd been locked in Randall's trunk again. Scrappy dispensed with the rules and leaped onto the bed, trying his best to lick away her nightmare.

Vivienne comforted her and fixed them both a cup of midnight tea until Penny was able to try to sleep again. Resolved not to awaken Vivienne a second time, Penny focused on lying still, staring at the ceiling and trying desperately to keep her mind on open-house details. Her brain would not stay on track. It was only when her thoughts drifted to Tyler and Rain and their joyful dinner party that she finally relaxed into sleep.

On Monday morning, she made her bed, brushing off the dog hair that accumulated when Scrappy rushed to comfort her in the middle of the night. They had declined maid service, which was just fine with Penny since it gave her something to do. She was desperate to get to the office. She'd carefully pulled her hair into a loose ponytail and dotted a bit of makeup over the worst of her facial bruises, as well as a swish of light pink lipstick.

"At least it's convenient for us to get to work from here," she told Vivienne when she emerged.

Vivienne shoved her short black hair behind her ears. "Absolutely, and we have a great view of the street, easy to keep an eye on things."

Vivienne reached into a paper bag and pulled out a bagel. "Want one? Caleb got bagels. He delivered them while you were in the shower."

Caleb Black, Vivienne's fiancé, not Tyler. She felt a stab of disappointment.

She was about to say "no thank you," but instead she nodded. Food was fuel, she told herself, and she needed fuel to do her job. "Maybe just a half. Thank you."

She managed to eat half a bagel with some strawberry cream cheese by the time Vivienne had swallowed the last of hers.

"All right," Vivienne said, putting down her phone. "Got the all-clear. We're safe to take the back exit and head to the office."

Thrilled to the core, Penny clipped a

leash on Scrappy and the two dogs followed them out of the hotel room. After a quick stop at the dog run, they arrived at the parking lot, where they found Tyler waiting.

Penny's pulse ticked up a notch, but at the same time the tension in her stomach dissipated a fraction. She recalled the warmth of his touch as she'd sat in the patrol car, wrists still smarting where Randall's duct tape had imprisoned her, the kiss on her knuckles… Tyler had been so kind, his blue eyes brimming with tenderness. Or perhaps it was just professional concern.

She offered a smile, but Tyler seemed nervous, detached. *I'm just a job*, she reminded herself, and Tyler was her brother's good friend, to boot. He was her cop babysitter, not anything more. The thought left a cold spot in the pit of her stomach. Their evening together with Rain had clearly not meant the same to him as it had to her. Vivienne drove her to the station with Tyler following in his vehicle.

When they arrived, she made a beeline for the kitchen, relived to find it empty as she set about making the coffee. Scrappy stayed close throughout the morning. Bradley and Tyler were on their phones, similar frowns etched on their faces. She knew they were chasing down leads at the local clinics and hospitals. The boat had been found within five minutes of her rescue. Randall had climbed into the back of a tarp-covered truck and escaped completely unnoticed, even by the driver, until he leaped out at an intersection and bolted.

She pictured Randall running at her with his knife raised over his head and her hands shook as she poured a glass of water in the kitchen. She was surprised to see Tyler's mother and Rain walk past toward the conference room. She put down her water and hurried to see them.

Francine beamed a smile. "Well, hello, Penny. Look, Rain. It's Miss Penny."

Rain waved a chubby hand. Penny sank to one knee and greeted her. "What are you two doing here?"

"Tyler said Dr. Gina was bringing Brooke and her puppies for a visit and who could resist a chance to see them?" Francine said.

Gina, the department veterinarian, had been taking care of Brooke and her puppies at the training center until the ownership issue was decided. Since the German-shepherd mother and pups had been found at the construction site, the whole unit had taken an interest in the canine family. Unfortunately, so had a man named Joel Carey, who insisted the dogs were his and intended to produce proof to that effect.

Penny had seen Joel at the station, loudly and brashly demanding his dogs be returned. She'd developed an instant dislike for the guy. Part of her hoped Joel wouldn't be able to prove the valuable dogs were his.

Penny made to follow Rain and Francine to the conference room, but Rain stopped her, arms raised, a bag of goldfish crackers in one hand.

Francine laughed. “I think she wants a lift. Better your back than mine.”

Penny hoisted Rain, who immediately twined her fingers in Penny’s hair. The heft of the child in her arms felt so sweet that Penny gave her a squeeze. Rain responded by resting her cheek against Penny’s shoulder. It awakened in Penny a deep satisfaction, which startled her. She had never allowed herself to really contemplate mothering before. The subject of lasting relationships and children inevitably raised feelings of sadness, disappointment and neglect. Penny had decided early on that she would not risk imposing those feelings on a child. There might be something deep down in her DNA, a strand of genetic selfishness, that would reveal itself if Penny had children, as it had in her own mother.

Perhaps that was why she always broke things off before they could get serious. The thought was too exhausting to entertain at that moment. She snuggled Rain closer. It was okay to dote on the little girl because there was no developing relationship with her father. The notion gave her an odd prick of both regret and relief.

As they walked along, Scrappy fell in behind. A low chuckle made them all turn. Tyler was walking a few paces after them, sporting a wide grin. The smile lifted the corners of his vibrant blue eyes and her heart did an unexpected dance.

"Scrappy's catching those fishy crackers in midair," Tyler said. "Best game ever."

Penny realized that Rain had been sprinkling a trail of crackers behind them for Scrappy to snarf down. She and Francine laughed, too.

"No wonder Scrappy loves Rain so much," Francine said. "She's like a vending machine for canines. I'm just going to pop into the ladies' room for a minute. I'll find you in a bit."

When she left, Tyler shot Penny an uncertain look. "Do you want me to take her? She can get heavy after a while."

"I'm happy to carry her." Penny blushed. Was he uncomfortable with her caring for Rain? Doubts assailed her. He knew how her mother had treated her. Maybe he thought she'd be like that with Rain. Maybe…

"Great," Tyler said, and his expression grew warm and relaxed.

She let loose a sigh. "I like hanging out with Rain. It takes my mind off things, and I think we're buddies now."

"Buddies for sure. I couldn't pick a better one for her." She searched his face for any clue that he was insincere, but she did not find any.

He moved nearer and pressed a kiss to Rain's head, which brought his mouth close to Penny's. She imagined for a moment that he lingered there, his lips so near hers.

Snap out of fantasyland. She soldiered on down the hallway, heart beating hard against her ribs.

They strolled into the conference room. Brooke and her puppies were enjoying pets and coos from the gathered officers. Scrappy sprinted to the nearest puppy, head down, bottom up, and began a playful tussle. Rain asked to be put down and was soon swarmed by two big-eared pups. Their button noses twitched in excitement and Rain's hearty giggle made Penny chuckle, too.

She and Tyler watched the canine chaos.

"I'm glad I got to see Rain today." Tyler sighed. "I'm away too much."

Penny had heard from Vivienne that Tyler had spent almost all of Sunday, his day off, at the station trying to track Randall Gage.

"I'm… I mean, well, I was going to

ask you if you'd made any progress, but I know you'd tell me if you could."

He grimaced. "Matter of time. Randall must have gotten help at a clinic somewhere. There was a fair amount of blood in the back of the truck he hitched a ride in. He was bleeding too heavily to patch himself up. I have a strong hunch, but the doctor I need to talk to had a family emergency. Waiting for a call back. I..."

He stopped at a wail from Rain. One of the puppies had gotten overenthusiastic and nipped her finger with needle-sharp teeth.

Penny immediately dropped to her knees. She took Rain's fingers in her palm and gently rubbed them. "There, see? I rubbed the ouchie away."

After a minute, Rain nodded and let Penny dab her tears with a tissue before she wriggled loose to resume her play with the puppies. Tyler extended a hand and helped up Penny. When she stepped on a dog toy and wobbled, he brought her steady against him with an arm around her waist.

"Where did you learn how to do that?" he said.

Her breath caught at the feel of his arm encircling her. "Do what?"

"That ouchie trick with Rain."

Penny stopped dead. Her heart squeezed as she struggled to reply. "My mother used to do that. I hadn't remembered until just this moment."

His face softened. "That's a nice memory."

"It is, isn't it?" The lump in her throat refused to budge. "I guess that means…"

"That she loved you."

Those three words hovered there.

She loved you.

And Randall's words chased behind them. *Your parents were terrible. They didn't care about you. Left you and your brother in dirty clothes, without regular meals, and they forgot about you at day care. Who forgets about their own child?*

She bit her lip and his hold fell away, except for his hand on her wrist. "Randall said they were bad parents, and he was right."

His tone was feather-soft when he spoke. "But they weren't bad parents because you were a bad child. I have thought about this topic a lot, you know, since Diane walked away from us. Someday Rain will come to me and ask why her mommy left. I will tell her that Diane didn't leave because there was something bad about Rain."

He caught her gaze, an earnestness on his face that made her reel.

Long-ago hurts flickered through her mind like an old-time slide show. Her parents had neglected her, forgotten her, left her craving love and acceptance, and she'd been worried that she was unlovable.

But here was this sweet and unexpected memory, her mother's tender touch, her desire to comfort. So what was the truth? The words echoed the question she'd asked God so many times.

Did they really love me?

She realized Tyler was watching her, one hand come to settle lightly on her shoulder. She blinked back into the present.

He leaned close, his mouth near her ear. "You are lovable and loved because God says so. I tell Rain that every day and I think maybe you need to hear it, too." His fingers caressed her shoulder as his words warmed her heart.

How had he known that it was what she most deeply desired to hear? What she prayed about in the long nights when sleep would not come? The wonder of it traced a warm path through her veins. She blinked against sudden tears.

You are lovable and loved because God says so.

Bradley strode in, face steely, and Tyler pulled away. Bradley jerked his chin at Tyler and they moved to a corner, talking urgently.

Penny forced herself to keep her attention on Rain. Whatever they were discussing was only going to cause her more tension. She retrieved a rubber ball from the corner and rolled it back into the wriggling pile of doggies. In truth, she wanted nothing more than to think about what Tyler had said, to turn it over and over as if she was holding a translucent gem up to the sunlight and watch it tease apart the glorious rainbow of colors.

Tyler returned to her, jaw tight. “I’ve got to go. Can you make sure Rain gets back with my mom?”

“Of course.” She clasped his arm as he turned to leave. “Is it about Randall?”

He covered her fingers with his just for a moment. “Yes, it’s the lead I was waiting for. I’ll keep you posted.”

She didn’t say all of the things that throbbed in her heart just then. *I’m afraid for you and my brother. Randall is a monster. Be safe.* Instead she nodded and moved closer to Rain. She couldn’t do a thing to stop Randall herself, but she could take care of Tyler’s little girl and say some silent prayers that this time, Randall would be stopped once and for all.

Tyler fought to keep his excitement in check as they hurried to their cars with the dogs.

"Doctor at a clinic right here in Bay Ridge finally got back to us," Bradley said. "She treated a guy matching Randall's description on Saturday night. Stitched up the wound on his side and provided antibiotics. He said his name was Aaron Fisher, but he was acting squirrelly so she covertly took a picture."

Bradley held up his phone so Tyler could see. The picture was blurry and dark, but it was clearly Randall Gage.

"Yes," Tyler said, adrenaline surging. "Finally."

Bradley continued. "He gave the doc an address in Bay Ridge that doesn't exist, but she remembered when she was locking up she heard him telling a taxi to take him to a location in Sunset Park."

It was the break they had been waiting for.

Tyler and Dusty followed Bradley's vehicle to a quiet street on the outskirts of the neighborhood. They stopped at the address the doctor had overheard, where a large four-story apartment building sat on the corner of an intersection. They found the building manager to be a young woman with a smile full of crooked teeth and a bright blue streak in her blond hair.

She considered their question. "Aaron Fisher? Yeah, he's lived here a while. I haven't seen him for a couple of days, but that's not unusual. He kept to himself. Not particularly outgoing."

"Do you have a phone number for him?"

She hesitated. "Is he in some kind of trouble?"

"Would you please call it, ma'am?" Tyler asked. "Right now."

A gleam of worry came into her eyes but she dutifully dialed the number. "No answer."

"Ma'am," Bradley said, "we are going

to need you to open the door for us, if he doesn't answer our knock."

"I don't think I should do that. Privacy is—"

Bradley cut her off. "We have reason to believe he's murdered two people, maybe more. We can get a search warrant if we need to, but time is critical."

She blanched, swallowed and reached for a key. "I'll open it." They followed her to the last unit at the end of a dark hallway.

Tyler directed the woman to step few feet away from the door. He put Dusty into a sit next to her and pounded on the door. "Randall Gage? Police. Open up."

Silence.

He rapped harder.

"Open up right now or I'm sending the dog in," Bradley shouted.

Nothing.

He gestured for the women to unlock the door and then guided her out of the way. Bradley and Tyler drew their weapons. King was electric with excitement, quivering from ears to tail.

Tyler ticked off a count of three on his fingers and then shoved the door open with his boot. At Bradley's command, King barreled inside, tearing around the small studio apartment like a heat-seeking missile. Tyler and Bradley were right behind him. After a few moments, he sat dejectedly, tongue lolling. Tyler whistled to Dusty, who confirmed their suspicions that Randall was not there.

Nonetheless, Tyler and Bradley checked the small closet, the bathroom and under the bed until they were satisfied their quarry was not hiding.

"Clear," Tyler called to Bradley. Biting back his disappointment, he holstered his weapon and began to scan the littered kitchen counter. Boxes of empty takeout, soda cans and old newspapers covered the aged tile. An open pantry door displayed shelves empty except for a box of sugary cereal and some canned chicken soup. A kitchen drawer was partially open—there was a tattered folder with photos spilling out. Tyler pulled a pen from his pocket and eased open the drawer.

His insides jolted. Stomach knotted, he pulled on a rubber glove and laid the folder on the table, flipping it open. "Bradley, come look at this."

Bradley joined him in an instant. They stood there for a moment in silence, perusing the dozens of newspaper clippings, yellowed with age.

Killer Clown Slays Two

Killer Leaves Little Girl Alive at Murder Scene

Slaying Investigation Goes Cold

"He must have clipped every mention he could find. Sick." Bradley's fists clenched as he studied the photos. Tyler counted fifteen, all pictures of Penny. Some had been cut from newspapers. One had been printed from the internet, an image of her sitting in attendance amid dozens of cops at the opening of the K-9 command unit. She was smiling, clapping.

Bradley's face went scarlet. "He's been stalking her."

There were other photocopied photos from a few news articles—one had been written just after Lucy Emery's parents had been killed, on the anniversary of the McGregor murders. The offset quote was Penny's.

> Randall Gage is a monster and he needs to be behind bars.

One article had been stuck on the door with tacks. The paper was crisscrossed by angry black marks, slashes of permanent marker that had defaced Penny's image in the accompanying photo and left black streaks on the door, where his anger had overflowed. In the middle of it all, he'd plunged a knife so deep through her image that it was halfway into the wood.

Tyler felt as though his body was boiling from the inside out. Randall had taken so much from Penny and Bradley, but he would not be content with that. He wanted it all, down to her very last breath. The knife proclaimed that loud and strong.

"We'll get a team in here," Tyler said. "I'll take Dusty around the vicinity and see if she can get any traces."

But they both knew Randall had abandoned the apartment and would not be coming back. Since there was no sign of blood or bandages, he'd obviously come here, taken what he needed and cleared out after he'd gotten patched up at the doctor's office. His actions were getting bolder because he knew the cops were close and it was a matter of time before he was captured or killed.

Randall was getting more and more desperate to complete his mission.

And they had to stop him before he made Penny pay the ultimate price.

NINE

Penny finished her report that afternoon in spite of the anxiety crawling up her spine. Tyler stood a few feet behind her, arms folded, staring at a spot on the wall. It was all she could do not to plead with him to take a coffee break or go for a run. Anything to relieve his brooding silence. Tyler had curtly informed her that Randall had abandoned his apartment, but her instincts told her he'd left something behind, something that was too terrible for them to reveal. Whatever he and Bradley had found, neither of them intended to share it with her. What could have been so awful? Goose bumps marched up her arms.

Don't let your mind go there.

She would have preferred to stay later

than four o'clock to finish a few lingering tasks and shave a couple of hours off her mind-numbing hotel time, but Tyler was clearly itching to take her home. Perhaps he was looking forward to having his babysitting duties over for the day so he could return to his investigation work. She sighed, considering the long evening ahead with Vivienne. It was probably hard for Vivienne, too, since she no doubt would rather be spending time with Caleb, discussing wedding details.

As she gathered her purse and a box of materials she wanted to organize for the open house, the office phone rang. It was not in her nature to allow a call to go to voice mail when it would likely only take a few seconds to answer and forward to the correct party. Penny picked up the receiver. "Brooklyn K-9 Unit. How can I help you?"

"I know where you can find Ivan Holland."

She jerked. Ivan Holland? The gunrunner who had tried repeatedly to kill Officer Noelle Orton and her K-9 partner, Liberty? Holland had put a bounty on Liberty's head after they'd foiled two smuggling operations at Atlantic Terminal and he'd made good on his threats to enact revenge. Holland was an ax hanging over Noelle and Liberty's head.

Stomach tight, she gestured to Tyler, who was at her side in three strides. "Who is this, please?" she said. She was afraid putting him on speakerphone might cause him to hang up, so instead she held the receiver between them so Tyler could hear.

"Never mind who I am. Ivan Holland is the guy who tried to kill your police dog. He put a ten-thousand-dollar bounty on that mutt's head, right? You want him or not?"

She tried to ignore the feeling of Tyler's muscled shoulder against her arm as he craned to see the number and wrote it on a notepad. He signaled for her to keep the conversation going.

"So you have information about Ivan Holland's whereabouts?" A rumbling screech sounded in the background. "It would help if you would give your name, sir. Then I can route you to the appropriate person to handle your information."

"You don't need to know my name. Ivan's time is over. We're not working for him anymore."

"Sir, if you'd just—" Penny began.

"I'm tellin' you where you can find Ivan right now. He's—" The caller stopped talking abruptly.

Penny gripped the phone. "Are you there, sir?"

"I have to go."

The phone went dead.

Tyler was already dialing the number he'd written down. Penny could hear the phone ringing endlessly, but it did not go to voice mail. He disconnected, then made a second call.

"Noelle? Tipster just called in about Ivan Holland's location. Wouldn't give his name and the call was cut off." He huffed out a frustrated breath. "No, I don't know where he was calling from. The number is a cell phone."

Penny bolted to her feet. "I know where he called from."

Tyler stared. "What? How could you know that?"

She grinned. "That noise in the background. Did you hear it? It's the Cyclone roller coaster at Coney Island."

He quirked up an eyebrow. "Are you sure?"

"Completely. I used to beg Bradley to take me. Once we rode it three times in a row until I got sick to my stomach. That sound is unmistakable. That's where the tipster is right now." If the caller was telling the truth, it was also very likely where Tyler would find the fugitive the unit had been seeking for more than six months.

"Noelle, meet me at Coney Island. I need you to make the positive ID and keep your distance. I'll handle the bust with backup. We won't risk him going after you or Liberty one more time," Tyler added to Noelle before he disconnected.

Penny and Tyler ran with both dogs in tow to Tyler's car. "I'll drop you at the safe house on my way," he said after she climbed in.

She shook her head. "That will take too much time. You have to go now or Holland might get away. I don't want to stay here by myself since most everybody is busy elsewhere at the moment, so I'll go with you."

He gunned the engine. "I'm not taking chances with your safety. I'll stay here with you until..."

"Call Vivienne. Tell her to meet us at Coney Island. I'll stay in the car until she gets there or until you're done."

"No way, I can't—"

"Yes, you can," she snapped. He jerked a look at her, eyes wide, but she plunged on. "This department has more to do than searching for Randall and babysitting me.

Holland is a menace." In fact, he had murdered an informant, targeted Noelle and would have succeeded in killing Liberty if the dog had not been so well trained. She tipped up her chin and looked Tyler full in the face. "I'm not letting you risk a chance to catch this thug for my sake. We have to go right now."

His eyes were pained. "I can't..."

She squared off with him. "If I'm not safe in a locked police car in the middle of Coney Island with a seventy-pound dog on my lap, then I'm not safe anywhere. Drive, Detective," she insisted.

It seemed as if her command had left him stunned. After a long moment of hesitation, he flipped on the lights and siren. "Buckle up."

She already had. Surprised at her own forcefulness, she sat back in the seat and watched the road fly by. Tyler didn't look at her and she wondered if she'd offended him.

But she was right. There were more people that needed protection, besides her. If Ivan Holland got away because of her, she would not be able to stomach that. Clutching the door handle, she steadied herself as Tyler wove in and out of traffic on their way to Coney Island, squawking his siren to punch his vehicle through.

They pulled up to the boardwalk that divided the broad stretch of beach from the amusement rides and vendors. The place brought back memories for Penny, and she smiled in spite of the circumstances. Summertime and stolen days with her brother were some of her sweetest childhood recollections. Bradley had saved up his money and treated her when he could. They'd ridden every ride they could afford and stuffed themselves with Nathan's Famous hot dogs—hers smothered in mustard and the works for him. She'd never tasted anything as delicious as those greasy treats.

"Best thing ever?" Bradley had said, his own fingers sticky with condiments.

She'd nodded. "Best thing ever, best brother ever."

When Bradley's money ran out, they would walk on the shore, searching for shells cast up on the sand. He always constructed elaborate sand villages that she decorated with bits of driftwood and broken shells. Their sprawling structures inevitably garnered attention from the other beachgoers. Penny loved the beach just as much as the rides. There on the sand, no one cared if a person's clothes were too small or a kid's bangs were crooked after her teen brother had done his best to trim them. Moments at the beach were glorious and golden.

The beach and boardwalk were always magnets for families walking hand in hand or playing near the surf—mothers, fathers and their children. Funny how that had never bothered her on those long-ago days. She'd had Bradley and he was enough. He was the biggest blessing in her life. Randall's threat echoed ominously in her mind.

First you, then your brother.

Stroking Scrappy's thick fur for comfort, she resolved to do whatever Bradley or Tyler asked of her, anything that would help capture Randall and make sure Bradley would have a future.

The massive wooden Cyclone stood proudly at the corner of Surf Avenue and West 10th Street, as it had since it opened in 1927. Its arching ramps and twists were darkly silhouetted against the sky. How she'd squealed in delight over each heart-stopping drop. Noelle and Liberty had already arrived, and had parked on the street that was tucked between the monstrous coaster in front and Luna Park behind. Only two months before both areas would have been jammed with summer vacationers, enjoying the scorching temperatures, but now the area had far fewer visitors.

Before he got out, Tyler turned to her.

"I know, I know," she said before he could speak. "Stay in the car. Do not open the door under pain of death. Text you at the first whiff of trouble."

He paused and, after a moment, grinned. "Okay, yeah, that's what I was going to say and one more thing."

"What did I forget?"

"Nothing." Quickly he leaned over and pressed a kiss to her cheek.

She started, nerves tumbling. "What is that for?"

"I've been meaning to thank you for making Rain's ouchie all better." He fingered a lock of her hair that was draped over one shoulder. "Thank you. You are a very special woman."

Before she could say a word in response, he got out of the car. In a fog, she watched as Noelle handed him a plastic bag, which he opened to give Dusty a sniff. She knew it was an item from the warehouse where Ivan Holland had murdered someone who had informed on him. Dusty grew excited, tail lashing, and led Tyler in the direction of the boardwalk. Noelle and Liberty followed, Liberty's tail arcing through the air in unison with Dusty's.

Tyler's kiss still felt warm on her cheek. She put her hand there to convince herself she hadn't imagined it. He'd really kissed her? After she'd bossed him so terribly? When he'd thought of her as a child not too long before?

You are lovable and loved because God said so.

She realized that in the course of a few days she had glimpsed a whole new side of Tyler than she'd ever seen before. He was a gentle man, a father with a deep wound who was still able to comfort and minister to others. He was faithful. He was loving.

Loving? To her? He had probably meant nothing by the kiss—it was just an automatic gesture, some sort of token of friendship. But her stomach somersaulted, anyway, as if she was taking a ride on the mighty Cyclone again.

Unhappy with his confinement, Scrappy whined and crawled into her lap, peering out the window to see where Tyler and Dusty had gone. Penelope clasped her arms around his stout neck and strained to do the same. Was Ivan Holland out there somewhere, lying in wait for Tyler and Noelle? Or perhaps the tip had been some sort of planned ambush by Holland's enemies.

Breathing gone shallow, all she could do was watch and wait.

Tyler did not allow himself to think about anything but Dusty as she scurried from spot to spot on the wide, slatted boardwalk. If he had, he would have tried to puzzle out just what in the world he'd been thinking kissing Penny.

To his left, past the boardwalk railings, was a wide expanse of golden sand with only two hardy individuals building castles in the autumn temperatures. It reminded him that Rain's upcoming birthday plan was to go to the beach in spite of the season. To his right was a line of ride entrances intermingled with pizza and hot-dog establishments, gelato stands and souvenir vendors. The smell of popcorn filled the air.

He trailed Dusty, confident that nothing would derail her from her quarry. He'd called for backup on the way. Noelle was scanning the crowd. Since Tyler had never actually seen Holland face-to-face, he was counting on her to make the identification more quickly that he could from the photos he'd been shown. With her eyes and Dusty's tracking, they would get him if the tipster's information had been correct. The golden retriever's nose was working overtime trying to sort out Holland's scent from the millions of visitor trails crisscrossing the boardwalk. So intent was he on his dog that he almost didn't notice the towheaded boy who raced over to pet Liberty, oblivious to the Police Dog, Do Not Pet sign emblazoned on her harness. As Noelle tried to get between the boy and Liberty, Tyler looked for the mother. He suspected it was the woman so distracted paying for two hot dogs she hadn't realized her son had wandered off.

At that precise moment, Dusty whined and sat near a man with sunglasses perched on a metal bench. The man tried to look nonchalant, but Tyler saw his posture stiffen as he took in the police dog. Noelle's eyes widened as she signaled Tyler. No mistake. Holland's panicked look flicked from Dusty to Tyler and he shoved a hand in his coat pocket.

"Stop right there—police," Tyler called, drawing his weapon.

Holland leaped to his feet and darted behind an older woman, who looked up in surprise. At the sight of Tyler's weapon, she froze and let out a small scream.

The scream caused panic to ripple through the handful of visitors, who began to run in all directions. "Get down," Tyler shouted, but he lost sight of Holland behind the scurrying bystanders.

"Tyler." Noelle's voice was tight with tension. He spun to find Ivan Holland with his hand gripping the neck of the boy who had been on his way to pet Liberty. Holland had a gun pressed to the boy's head. Noelle restrained a barking Liberty with one hand and gripped her revolver in the other.

The mom turned toward the commotion, dropped the hot dogs and shrieked. "Stay there," Tyler shouted at her. "Holland, let the kid go," he commanded.

Holland's eyes thinned to slits. "No way. One of my people tipped you off, huh? Traitor."

Tyler took a step forward. The mother was sobbing now.

"Please, let him go," she wailed. "Don't hurt my son."

Out of the corner of his eye, Tyler saw two cops making their way along using the row of trash cans as cover. A couple steps closer and Holland would be surrounded, but the area was a target-rich environment with plenty of potential for injuries or worse.

"I'll kill this boy if you try to stop me from leaving," Holland yelled.

"You don't want to do that," Tyler said. "Let him go and we'll talk it over."

"Nothing to talk about. I walk or the kid dies." Holland gave the boy a shake. Tears coursed down the youngster's face.

"Stop," his mother sobbed. "You're hurting him."

One of the newly arriving cops reached an arm out to keep her from coming any closer, but she lurched around him and rushed at Holland. Holland instinctively stepped back, stumbling as he did so. Tyler sprang at Holland and knocked him over backward, away from the child. The gun tumbled loose from his grip. Noelle was there in a flash, kicking the weapon away and training her own weapon on the gunrunner.

The mother scrambled to her son, clutching him, tears streaming down her face.

Holland struggled, but Tyler overwhelmed him easily, rolling him onto his stomach. Dusty and Liberty were both barking up a storm. The man grunted and thrashed.

"Shoulda killed that dog," Holland spat, his cheek pressed to the dirty boardwalk.

"Now you'll never get the chance." As Tyler cuffed and Mirandized him, he felt a surge of intense satisfaction. Finally they had one fugitive in custody. Next on the agenda was putting the killer clown away for life.

Cops closed in from behind, keeping the crowd back and securing the loose weapon.

Breathing hard, Tyler looked up at Noelle with a grin. "About time, huh?"

She grinned back at him and lowered her weapon. "My thoughts exactly." She rubbed Liberty's ears. "Looks like the target is off our backs, sweetie." Liberty celebrated with a long lick to her partner's face.

Tyler and Noelle both took a moment to get their breathing under control and wipe the sweat from their brows. Adrenaline still swamped his senses, but he calmed as he rewarded Dusty with her favorite rope-pull toy and they enjoyed a quick game of tug. He tossed it for her, and she happily chased it down. Another job well done, another bad guy going to prison, where he belonged.

Tyler and Noelle waited until Holland was safely loaded into the back of a police car, and made sure the boy was not injured. To be on the safe side, they'd called in a medic to check over both the boy and the mother. Noelle arranged a ride for them back to the station to give their statements.

"That was scary, and I didn't even get to

go on any rides," the boy said, face crumpling.

The dad in him pitied the disappointed child. "Well, how about if I ask the officer to show you the red lights and sirens on his car? How about that?" Tyler suggested. "He might even let you turn them on yourself."

The child's eyes lit up. Tyler escorted them to the waiting police car and asked the officer to take special care of his juvenile transport. Tyler heard the boy's enthusiastic chatter as the cop bent to talk to him.

Overhead the squeals of delight carried from the Cyclone, as passengers plunged down a turn at sixty miles per hour. The thought occurred to him that it had been far too long since he'd ridden the big wooden attraction. The last time was when he and Diane were dating. At the top of that roller coaster, he'd looked out over the ocean and thought his future was right on track with the woman he loved. Then there had been the gut-twisting plunge. He'd not been back to Coney Island since that day, and he'd thought he would never return. All of a sudden he found he was looking forward to giving it another try. Rain would love the colors and excitement, and someday she'd be big enough that he could take her on the Cyclone, too.

An unexpected thought intruded. What would it be like if Penny was with them, her red hair streaming out behind her against the blue sky? They'd share some cotton candy as pink as her cheeks and listen to Rain's squeals together, like a couple in love, a family. What? The daydream burst as quickly as it had formed, leaving him reeling.

His mind was giving out on him. First he'd kissed Penny. Now he was imagining family trips and thinking about love? What was the matter with him? Marriage was not some fairy tale and he was nowhere near wanting to enter into that tumultuous adventure anytime soon. Rain was more than enough of a challenge.

He shook his head and took a moment to gather himself.

"You okay?" Noelle asked.

"Perfect, just decompressing."

She nodded and headed for her vehicle.

In a few more moments, he made his way to his car with Dusty. As he drew closer, he considered Penny's command that he drive immediately to Coney Island. She had not sounded anything like an uncertain young girl. That was Penny McGregor at her strongest.

And at her most attractive. She was looking at him now through the car window, eyes wide. He recalled the feel of her satin cheek against his lips. The massive post-adrenaline reaction was getting to him, had to be. He did his best to push the thoughts away as he strode closer to his vehicle and opened the back door.

"Did you get him?" she asked.

"We sure did."

Penny's squeal of delight lit up his senses. That feeling came over him as he let Dusty climb in, the stomach-clenching sensation of being at the precipice of the roller coaster, ready for the drop. Teeth gritted, he willed away the feeling.

Been there, done that. Not doing it again.

He got inside and closed the door, firmly sealing out the noise of the giant roller coaster.

TEN

Penny was elated as they drove back to the safe house. Tyler's report about Holland's capture was no doubt missing many details, but she was thrilled that the gunrunner was in custody and there had been no injuries. Noelle and Liberty deserved some peace of mind. She wondered why Tyler did not look as happy as she felt. After a few quiet minutes rolled by, she asked, "Is something wrong?"

He shrugged. "Not really. I was just thinking about that boy. An act of violence like that can really mess up a child." He froze, jerking a glance at her. "Uh, I wasn't talking about you, Penny."

Her face burned. Is that what he saw? A grown-up version of a messed-up kid?

It was exactly the opposite of what she'd worked her whole life to prove to herself, that she was not defined by what had happened to her at the age of four. "It's okay. You're right. Violence does damage children—adults, too. I'll pray for him." She fastened her gaze out the window.

"I don't think of you that way, damaged by what happened to you." His voice was soft and it drew her back to him, but the hurt remained.

"You probably don't think of me at all." Why had those words come out of her mouth? Like she was some self-pitying teen? Aghast, she knotted her fingers together and stared at her lap.

He sighed, low and quiet. "Oh, but I do. Lately I can't stop thinking about you."

Thinking about her? Did he mean the case? Randall's threats? But the gentle blue of his eyes made her feel that he was not referring to police work. "I guess the Randall case is on everyone's mind," she finally said.

"It's not the case, Penny." He cleared his throat. "You aren't who I thought you were."

"How so?"

He rubbed a hand over tired eyes. As his body relaxed from the tense situation with Holland, his defenses seemed to ease, as well, and his words came tumbling out. "I don't know, exactly. I've learned lately that I have a bad habit of putting people into boxes rather than finding out who they really are. I've been guilty of it since my marriage ended. Maybe it's a form of self-protection or a cop trait. I mentally boxed you up in the too-young category."

"Too young for what?"

He looked out the window, at his steering wheel, fiddled with the radio. "Ah, um, friendship, you know, or…things."

"Things?" It was not her imagination. He was flushed an embarrassed red.

Suddenly he looked as awkward as a teenager who'd tripped over his own feet. "Not that I'm in the market for…things, right now. I mean, Rain and I are doing great. I've got her and my job, so that's really all I can handle. But if I was, you know, well, I mean if the situation was different, you are the type of woman I would, uh…" He thunked his head against the headrest. "Can you please talk for a while so I can stop embarrassing myself?"

She laughed. "Sure thing. What should I talk about?"

"Anything, everything. Whatever you want so I can use my ears instead of my mouth."

"Okay," she said over her thudding pulse. "How about I tell you all my glorious plans for the office open house this weekend? That should be suitably boring." *And safe.*

"Excellent," he said, visibly relaxing. "I'm all ears."

Penny rattled on about the details, everything from the frosted fall leaf cookies to the coloring and dress-up activities for the kids. The conversation lasted all the way to the hotel safe house, where Vivienne was waiting just inside the rear entrance to ensure the hallway was clear.

"Thank you," Penny said automatically as she got out of the car.

"I should be thanking you." Tyler's smile was rueful as he walked her in. "You allowed us to bag Holland, and you kept me entertained the whole way home."

She shrugged. "Happy to do my part."

"Sorry for running off at the mouth." Tyler bid her a formal good-night. He seemed uncomfortable, unhappy, perhaps, that he'd shared his thoughts with her. "You're a one in a million and I really admire you. That's what I was trying to say."

She blushed.

And then he bent to hug her and wrapped his arms around her waist, her cheek pressed close to his. "You just don't know how special you are, do you?"

Her breath caught as her face tipped up to his. He was angling his head to kiss her when Vivienne opened the door for her and Scrappy. Tyler instantly stepped away, looking at his boots. "Okay. Well, I'll see you tomorrow."

"Okey doke." When Penny turned to look over her shoulder, Tyler was already striding away.

You just don't know how special you are...

She realized she felt exactly the same way about him. Thoughts of Tyler would simply not leave her head. But were they talking about different things? He'd considered her too young, ruled her out as a friend. Or was he talking about something deeper?

How did he really feel?

And how did she?

Back in the hotel room, Vivienne locked up and Penny poured a bowl of kibble for Scrappy.

Vivienne laid some paper plates on the table and unbagged some deli sandwiches. "Sorry, it's deli again. I wish I knew how to cook. Caleb will tell you he'll be wearing the apron in our kitchen after we're married."

Penny laughed and took a bite of her turkey sandwich. "You already have those roles all worked out?"

Vivienne's eyes lit up. "We talk all the time. He's the most amazing man I've ever met, my best friend in the whole world. We have chemistry." She sipped some grape soda and eyed Penny over the top of the can. "You know, it seems to me that you and Tyler have some chemistry also."

Penny coughed and quickly gulped some soda. "Us? No, we're just..."

"Friends?"

"I'm not sure of that, even, let alone anything else."

Vivienne's eyes took on a mysterious glint. "Oh, I'm a pretty keen observer of human nature and believe me, Tyler finds you fascinating. I see the way he was looking at you at the puppy play date. He gets this dopey faraway expression when he's watching you. And what I interrupted there when I opened the door..." She grinned.

Penny's face went hot. "Oh, well, I believe he thinks I'm too young for him."

She waved a hand. "His brain might think so, but his heart is listening to an entirely different story. Trust me. I'm a whiz about these things."

Penny managed to get the conversation switched to easier subjects, but that night, curled up with Scrappy, she allowed herself one moment to imagine that Vivienne's scenario was real.

She and Tyler together, a family with Rain.

She'd never allowed herself to conceive of a future with anyone.

Was it time to let herself believe it?

Or was she setting herself up for the biggest heartbreak of her life?

With Randall ready to kill her at any moment, it was sheer foolishness to be contemplating relationships with Tyler or anyone else for that matter.

Tyler finds you pretty fascinating...

Smiling, she closed her eyes and let herself relax into sleep.

Tyler woke up Tuesday morning determined to keep his mouth in check. He couldn't imagine why being around Penny made him go soft in the head to the point that he began to babble. At the usual time, there was a soft knock and he opened the door for his mom.

"Good morning, Mom. Rain is ostensibly tidying her room, which means it will probably be a bigger mess than it was before."

"We'll sort it all out. Are you going to see Penny today?" she said. "Can you invite her over for dinner maybe?"

He sighed. Might as well take the bull by the horns. "Mom, I know you've got your hopes up, but Penny and I are not in a relationship."

She hung her coat on the back of the chair. "You could be, if you wanted to."

"There are way too many obstacles between us."

"Mostly just one big obstacle, Ty, namely you."

"It's a bad idea."

She fixed him with an intense look. "Things didn't work out with Diane. That hurt you deeply, but you are meant to keep running the race, honey. God doesn't want you to seal yourself off from the love He puts into your life."

He felt his cheeks go hot. "I'm not sure God has put Penny in my path as a love interest, Mom."

"All due respect, Ty, but you are not always a fount of wisdom."

He jerked. "What?"

"Well, remember the time you let Rain take a brush to bed and it wound up so tangled in her hair we had to cut it out?"

"Yes, but..."

"And the enchiladas you forgot about in the back of your SUV for three days?"

He sighed. "Uh-huh."

"And the day you thought it would be a great idea to replace the—"

"All right." He held up his palms. "I get your point, but right now I have to hit the road. Vivienne had to go out on an assignment with Hank so I'm Penny's transport." He swiftly kissed her on the cheek. "Talk to you later. Let's go, Dusty."

"But Ty..."

He rushed out the door before she had a chance to formulate her follow-up questions.

His mother was well-meaning, but she didn't understand. It was his responsibility to protect Penny, not love her. Or was his mom correct and he was merely trying to protect himself from risking his heart again?

He picked up Penny up at the hotel and drove them to the K-9 Unit firmly committed to keeping things professional.

Shoving aside his mother's words, he felt like his head was screwed on straight until the moment he ushered Penny and the two dogs into the police-department lobby. Penny stepped behind him and took something from his back pocket.

He looked in horror at a pair of fuzzy pink bunny ears, then snatched them up.

"You..." Penny started giggling. "This was in your pocket." She'd hardly managed to get the words out in between bouts of laughter that transformed her into the most breathtaking creature he'd ever seen.

Embarrassment warred with delight. Her laughter was exquisite, like water bubbling over river rocks. "Uh, Rain insisted we play dress-up this morning. I had to be the bunny." He groaned. "I can't believe I forgot to take it out of my pocket." She was still overwhelmed by giggles, and he found himself laughing along with her.

"I get it," she said. "Anything for Rain."

He chuckled some more. "Nothing is

more humbling to the male ego than raising a daughter."

"You're a good dad. Real men aren't afraid to wear pink bunny ears," she said when her own giggles subsided.

Caleb strolled in checking a text on his phone. He did a double take at the bunny ears in Tyler's hand. He arched an eyebrow. "Are you working on a new look, Walker?"

Penny quickly took the ears and put them on her own head. "Just trying out something for the dress-up box for the kiddie corner at the open house. How do I look?"

"Fantastic," he said. "Those ears are perfect on you. Talk to you two later."

Tyler let out a breath as Caleb left. "Thanks for the save. He would never let me live it down if he knew I was carrying around pink ears in my back pocket and dressing up like a rabbit in my off hours."

"I guess you owe me one, Detective."

He reached over and tweaked the costume ears. "I guess I do." He willed the thought into words. "I, uh, I was wondering if maybe, you know, after we capture Randall, if you would like to go on an adventure with me and Rain. A museum trip, or maybe a kiddie movie or something like that." There. He'd asked her out on a date, sort of.

She gave him that incandescent smile. "I think that would be great."

"Great." He felt the silly grin spread across his face, but he could not wipe it away.

Penny took off the ears and headed for the coffee room. Tyler followed, feeling as if he was floating. She soon had the place smelling of fresh-brewed coffee and three cops were in line at the machine.

"We're here for your special pumpkin-spice blend, Penny," Lani said. "The weekend cops complain that they have to make do with plain old java on your days off."

"I'll have to try a weekend shift someday." Lani's eyes widened as Penny pulled a plastic container from her bag and transferred some goodies to a plate. "I had a batch of blondies in the freezer at home. Vivienne drove over and retrieved them for me."

Tyler noted in awe that the cops closed in for the sweets like moths to a porch light.

"Thanks, Penny," Raymond Morrow said. "I'm taking one for now and one for later."

"Aww, man. Love me some blondies," Henry Roarke added.

"Blondies?" Jackson Davison said, sticking his head in. "I'm just in time."

By the time Tyler finished pouring his coffee, every last treat was gone. "You guys are vultures," he called in mock outrage. "I didn't even get one measly treat."

"Snooze, you lose," Henry said, retreating to his desk.

Tyler's stomach grumbled, reminding him he'd skipped breakfast to get in that game of dress-up with Rain. He sat glumly at the table until Penny slid a napkin in front of him with a fat blondie in the center.

He blinked at the treat. “You saved me one?”

She nodded. “You need your strength for the next round of dress-up.”

He laughed and took a big bite of the blondie, then rolled his eyes at the chewy pleasure. “And to think I might have missed out on this if you hadn’t had my back.”

Penny shrugged. “I don’t like anyone to be left out.”

Yet he hadn’t seen her set aside treats for any other cop. She was giving him special consideration. *Gratitude for shuttling her around, probably, you dope.* But she’d said yes to a future date with him. Or maybe she’d only agreed because she liked his daughter? He sat staring at the blondie.

Darcy Fields entered and inhaled. “The

smell of coffee is the only thing that got me out of an endless meeting. If the lab had coffee like this, I would probably never leave for any reason." She helped herself to a cup and sat at the table. "I'm so close to a breakthrough I can taste it."

Tyler straightened. He knew exactly what she was referring to. The forensic scientist had been tirelessly working to capture some DNA left at the Emery crime scene. Darcy would provide the definitive answer to the question they'd all been wondering.

Had Randall Gage killed the Emerys, too? Or did they have another killer at large?

He motioned for Penny to join them. "We're really counting on you, Darcy. I've gotten nowhere with Lucy's clue about the elusive friend named Andy, and Randall so far has not given us anything conclusive related to the second killings. It's looking like you're our only hope until he's in custody and confesses the way he did to Penny about her parents' murders. If he even is the Emerys' killer."

Darcy grimaced. "I'm working as fast as I can, but science is slow."

Penny patted her hand. "My brother always says you have to go slow to go fast."

"My slow pace is not going to be good enough if he gets close to you again. I heard what happened at the docks. Are you okay?"

Penny's smile was bright but forced. "Just a little banged up, is all. Tyler got there just in time." He saw the brave front she presented to Darcy, but the clenching of her hands gave her away. That cheerful demeanor did not completely hide the fear written underneath, not from him, anyway. It made him burn with urgency to neutralize Randall before he could inflict any more agony on the McGregors.

Nate Slater poked his head in the break room. "Some boxes delivered for you, Penny. They're stacked in the front office."

"On my way. Must be the tablecloths I ordered for the open house."

Tyler finished his coffee and put the mug in the dishwasher. "I'll help you move them."

She didn't decline his assistance and he was oddly pleased. He hefted the larger of the two cartons and she scooped up the smaller one with her name scrawled in black on top. "We'll just put them in the conference room until I get them sorted out."

They delivered the boxes. As much as he enjoyed staying with Penny, it was time to start another round of phone calls to follow every last clue he could that would lead him to Randall's whereabouts. "See you later."

"For sure." She waved the bunny ears at him. "What should I do with these?"

"Bring them over next time you come to play." He was out of the room before he wondered what she thought of his casual invitation. Would she think he was using her as a source of free babysitting for Rain? Flirting?

Was he flirting? He wasn't sure he even knew how.

He was a complete mess, he thought as he rubbed a hand over his forehead. Dusty greeted him with a tail wag from her cushion near his desk, but she didn't get up. "Maybe you and I need some exercise time to clear our brains, huh?"

Something niggled at his gut as he grabbed her leash. Dusty was up, alive with excitement. He laughed at her exuberance, but there was still a nagging detail deep down in his gut that refused to surface.

What was it?

He paused in the doorway, sifting through the details of the morning.

Bunny ears.

Packages.

Black marker.

His nerves fired. Black marker. It was

probably nothing. *Check it out, anyway.* "Come on, girl," he said to Dusty.

He headed toward the conference room and as they got closer, Dusty's nose quivered. Two more steps and she pulled on the leash, eager to get to the scent—an old scent she'd remembered from before.

The scent left by Randall Gage and his black marker.

"Penny," Tyler shouted as he ran. "Don't open that box!"

ELEVEN

Penny tore open the cardboard flap at the same moment she heard Tyler's shouted warning. She screamed as a puppet exploded from the box. The crude felt figure reached the end of its spring and recoiled. Torn paper shreds flew out and fluttered to the carpet. Reeling, she fell onto the floor.

Scrappy shoved his concerned nose in her face. She clung to him, trying to understand what had just happened. Dusty raced in and sat, posture stiff to show she'd found a target. Tyler was next, blue eyes absorbing the scene before he sank to a knee at her side. Taking her elbow, he scooted her away from the settling debris until she was sitting with her back against the wall. The solid surface behind her kept her grounded.

Tyler looked over his shoulder and moved slightly, blocking her view of what had sprung from the box.

She gulped in a breath. “I want to see it,” she said, craning her neck.

“I don’t think…”

She gritted her teeth, the fear whipping her pulse into a frenzy. “Tyler, don’t try and protect me from the truth. This is my place of work, it’s my life, and I want to see what he’s done.” Her forceful tone sounded as if it was coming from someone else’s mouth.

He studied her for a minute and then nodded. “All right.” As he moved aside, she could properly make out the hideous contents of the package. Her senses reeled as she took it in. The puppet was still waving slightly from side to side on the spring. Where the facial features should have been was a cut-out photocopied picture of Penny’s face. It must have been taken at a happy time in her life, she thought. She was smiling, the collar of her desk clerk uniform shirt showing. Perhaps she'd just gotten her job with the police department. Her eyes roamed the grotesque toy's body, which was covered with splotches of brilliant red paint. It took her a moment to realize the symbolism. The red was meant to resemble blood…her blood.

Randall's promise made visual.

In case she didn't get that message clearly, he'd made one more addition. She swallowed as she examined the rope noose strung around the puppet's neck. Scrappy poked at her leg with his wet nose, whining softly. She absently caressed his ears and held him close to keep him away from the macabre delivery.

Gavin arrived at a run, eyes wide, and from somewhere far away she heard Tyler explaining what had happened.

"I should have noticed earlier," Tyler said. "The black marker was similar to what we found in Randall's apartment.

Dusty picked up his scent on the package as we got closer to the conference room."

Their words faded away as she looked down at the torn papers on the floor. What she'd mistaken for newspaper scraps were actually photocopied pictures of her, but the eyes were poked out and the papers were torn into pieces.

It should have been fear, she felt then, but instead it was a fountain of anger that bordered on rage, unlike anything she'd felt before. Randall's evil had invaded her place of work, her lone sanctuary, the hub of her cop family. She turned on Tyler. "What did you find at his apartment?"

He looked as though he was about to try to put her off the topic. Then he reconsidered. "Pictures of you, defaced, like this. Newspaper clippings of your parents' murders." He paused. "A photocopy of the interview when you called him a monster."

She got to her feet with a hand from Tyler. "He's been planning his revenge carefully, hasn't he? He's invaded every area of my life, even here."

Gavin cleared his throat. "Penny, I am going to ask something of you now that you're not going to like."

She braced herself. "You're sending me home, aren't you?"

He held up a placating hand. "Just for today, until we run down how this package was delivered here and set some things in place."

Her rage flared, high and bright. "So now he gets to take my job from me, too? He's stripped me of my home, my security and now this?"

"It's the safest choice," Tyler said.

Gavin patted her arm. "Just for today, okay? Let us do our jobs here and make sure our security is shored up so we can keep you and everybody here safe. Do you understand?"

And everybody here. It occurred to her just then that if Randall had sent a bomb or a chemical poison, everyone in the building might have been affected. It wasn't just about her anymore. She swallowed and willed herself to speak.

"Yes, sir," she said, hardly able to say the words. "I understand."

"All right. Tyler, take her back to the secure room at the hotel, and I'll alert Vivienne to meet you there. Staff meeting in one hour. I'll get people in here to photograph this mess before we clean it up." He looked at Penny again. "I promise. I'll have you back at work before you know it."

Penny didn't reply. She could not be certain the anger wouldn't burst from her just as the puppet had exploded from the box. Silently, she followed Tyler and Dusty to the squad car. Scrappy seemed to pick up on her emotional morass. His ears were down as he climbed into the vehicle. She felt Tyler sneaking glances at her, but he did not try to make small talk as they made their way back to the safe house.

"Vivienne will be here in twenty. I'll

take you up and stay until she arrives, okay?"

Penny managed a nod. Back in her dreary hotel room, she could not force herself to sit. Instead she paced laps around the dingy carpet while Scrappy whined from his lookout post on the couch.

Tyler rubbed his palms on his pants. "Can I, uh, make you some tea or coffee or something? I know how to prepare beverages, at least."

She didn't even have the energy to force a smile. "No thank you."

"Penny…"

"This isn't fair." The words catapulted from her mouth. He jerked, startled.

His reply was gentle. "That's true. Not one single thing about this is fair."

"Why does Randall have the right to take so much from me?" Her voice was loud, echoing in the bare room. "My parents, my home, my job. What makes him so special that he can turn me into a victim for my entire life? How does he have that right?" She was almost shouting now, her fingernails biting into the palms of her clenched fists.

"He doesn't."

"But he's doing it, Tyler." Her eyes filled. "One day at a time, he's stripping it all away and he's going to keep going until I've lost everything." She gulped. "He's going to kill me and then he's going to kill my brother." Her voice broke on the last word.

"No, he's not."

"How can you say that? He's still running around loose." Tears splashed hot down her cheeks. "And I'm the one locked up in a hotel room. It's not fair." Now the sobs came out of her along with the tears that she no longer attempted to staunch. "Is God punishing me?" The horrible question rose again from the darkest place in her soul. *Am I unlovable? Do I deserve this?*

He took hold of her shoulders and drew her to him. Her sobs shook her, but his arms were steady, stroking her back, pressing his cheek to the top of her head, repeating over and over.

"This is going to end."

How? When? The questions remained locked inside and all she could do was cry.

He held her until her sobs died away and she was left sniffling. "I shouldn't be yelling at you," she whispered, taking the tissues he handed her.

"Yell all you want. I'm glad you can share your feelings with me." His embrace was tender and strong, comforting and encouraging. She breathed in the scent of his aftershave, felt the strong beat of his heart next to her cheek. She had the oddest sense that she belonged there, pressed close to him, allowing herself to let go of a burden that had been building since she was a little girl.

When the storm of emotion eased, she was left with both a reservoir of fear and an odd feeling of comfort. How was it possible to have both? She wasn't sure, but she knew that Tyler's arms around her had brought her closer to hope, and farther away from despair.

"I'm sorry," she said.

He tipped up her chin to meet his eyes. "You don't have to be sorry. You can rage and cry and vent all you need to with me."

"You don't want to hear all that."

His finger caressed her chin. "I am privileged to hear all that."

Tiny flickers of light danced through her bloodstream at his touch. "I… Thank you." She felt her face flush. "You don't have to…"

And then he was pressing a kiss on her lips and everything flew away in the tender rush of comfort. She felt his hand skim the back of her hair as he let the kiss linger for a moment before he pulled away.

"You just remember what I told you, Penny. You are lovable because God made you that way. You just hang onto that and we'll do the rest. Randall will not rob you of the things you love. I won't allow it."

Oh, how she desperately wanted to believe it, to believe him. His kiss had been so precious, just like his words.

Vivienne's knock on the door made her jump. Tyler cleared his throat, and let her in. After a brief conversation, he called for his dog, and then he was gone, leaving her to wonder at what had just passed between them.

Tyler grabbed a cup of coffee before heading to the meeting, hoping the strong brew would clear the buzzing from his senses. Every nerve in his body was at full alert. What had he done, kissing her like that?

You were comforting her, that's all.

But he knew it was a lie. Yes, he could not bear to see her distressed, but he'd also found himself comforted by that kiss. The oddest feeling percolated through him—the radical thought that Penny McGregor was meant to be his. The feeling was deeper and more profound than he'd ever experienced before, even with Diane.

Use your head, he warned himself. He began ticking off the reasons that anything more than a friendly relationship was a very bad idea indeed.

First of all, it was his job to protect her. He was a cop, and she was his duty. Period. Emotional attachments would only impede that. That was exactly why interoffice romances were discouraged.

Second, he was seven years older than Penny and the weary father of a child who'd already lost one mother. Dive deeply into another relationship now that Rain was old enough to form strong attachments? The thought of inviting a woman into their lives and then having her walk away was too much to consider. It would shatter his heart, but what would it do to a toddler to have a second mommy desert her?

Third…

Bradley's poke on his arm brought him

from his reverie. "I just talked to Penny. She said you calmed her down. Thanks, man."

Tyler smiled weakly. Reason number three screamed across his brain: Penny was his buddy Bradley's sister. Bradley was fiercely protective, as he should be. Cops should not date other cop's baby sisters.

Bradley frowned. "What's going on? You're off in space somewhere."

"Sorry." He gulped some coffee, which burned his tongue.

Gavin stood at the whiteboard as the officers took their seats. "All right. We know Randall mailed the package using a fictitious return address. I've gone over procedure with the mail room and all packages will be screened there before they're delivered to the office."

Henry gestured to his beagle. "They'll call me if any odd packages arrive and Cody will do an explosives check."

Explosives. Would that be Randall's

next attempt? Tyler noticed Bradley's jaw was tight.

"What leads to we have?" Gavin asked.

Caleb spoke up. "Got a possible tip putting Randall at a homeless shelter in Dyker Heights, but it looks like he cleared out, if that was him."

"Nothing further from the Emery crime scene?" Sarge asked.

Caleb shook his head. "Nothing conclusive until we get Darcy's DNA results."

"Nothing substantial on the Andy clue," Tyler said. "I'm half convinced Lucy's friend might be an imaginary one."

"So we still don't know if we're looking at one killer or two." The room went quiet at Gavin's words.

Tyler drummed his fingers on the table. "If Randall killed the Emerys also, why didn't we find many newspaper clippings about it at his apartment? There was only one. He'd practically built a shrine about the McGregor murders, particularly about Penny."

Bradley glowered. "He's obsessed with her."

"Or he hasn't had time to collect much on the Emery killings," Caleb added.

"In any case, time's ticking away. We need to bust Randall Gage before he makes good on his threats." Gavin looked at Bradley. "Probably wouldn't be a bad idea for you to go to a safe house also. This isn't just about your sister."

A vein in Bradley's jaw jumped. "No."

Tyler tried a cajoling tone. "Hey, man. Couple of days off with pizza and football to watch. Doesn't sound bad to me."

"I said no." Bradley's tone was clipped and hard. "I hope Randall comes after me. Better me than Penny because King and I are ready. He won't get a second chance."

Tyler wasn't surprised at Bradley's reaction. He'd have said something similar if it was his sibling on the line.

"Right, well the other item on the table is the fall open house on Saturday." Gavin leaned against the podium. "Makes most sense to cancel."

Cancel. That would be the final broken straw in Penny's life.

Gavin continued. "But that may not be necessary if we move all activities inside. We're getting some pressure from higher up to go forward with it so there will be photos and video clips to put on the web of our new command unit." He paused and cleared his throat. "They made the suggestion that we could go forward with the event while Penny is secured at the safe house."

There was an angry buzz around the table, but Tyler's voice rose the loudest.

"No way. Penny put her heart and soul into that open house. It's her event. If she isn't allowed to be here, we should cancel."

There were murmurs of agreement.

Gavin nodded. "That was my thought, as well. We can postpone the public-access segment for later in the year and continue on with the part which was intended for cops and cop families only. We'll know everyone on the guest list. No one gets past the front desk unless they're buzzed in. We can pull in some personnel on overtime and button this place down tight. Any objections?"

Tyler wanted to speak, but he knew it had to be a unanimous decision.

"Penny's worked so hard on it. I say we go forward," Henry said.

Gavin scanned the reactions from his officers. "All right. Let's vote on it. All in favor?"

Every person in the room raised their hands.

Tyler felt a swell of pride. All the cops in the unit respected Penny and wanted the best for her. She was one of their own. Her cop family would not allow Randall to strip this important day from her.

It was one small victory, but to her, it would be enormous.

He felt again the softness of her lips on

his, the strange buzz of bliss at being close to her.

Straightening in his chair, he reminded himself of his excellent reasons for avoiding a relationship with Penny.

Falling in love with her was out of the question right now.

If only his heart would fall into line.

TWELVE

Penny was nearly beside herself with excitement when Saturday morning finally rolled around. The days of her pseudo incarceration had crawled by in painful slow motion. She'd been awake for several hours already by the time Tyler arrived. Her hair was neatly secured in a twist and she wore her fall-hued sweater. Vivienne told her the burnt orange and golds complemented her coloring. She thought about that remark while she added a bit of pink to her lips and the tiny glass acorn earrings her adoptive mother had given her years before.

Tyler's weary eyebrows lifted in appreciation when he saw her. "You look great," he said.

"Oh, thank you," she said. He rubbed his eyes and she felt a small pang of guilt that she'd required such an early pickup when he'd been keeping long hours working on the hunt for Randall. "Still waking up?"

He waved a hand. "Naw, I'm fine." He smoothed a hand over his jaw. "But is it really necessary that we get to the office at six thirty when the party doesn't start until noon?"

"Sorry, but yes. I have a million things to do. Can I make it up to you with a good cup of coffee when we get there? I've got my own special blend ready to perk up a pot."

He smiled. "A good cup of coffee will get you plenty of forgiveness from this cop. Throw in a muffin and I'm your devoted servant for life."

"You need to get yourself one of these brownies," Vivienne said as she entered, holding up a napkin containing a half-eaten, gooey treat. "Wait until you taste these caramel thingies. Francine was a rock star to help out."

He gaped. "My mom baked these?"

Vivienne grinned. "Yes and no. I got Penny the ingredients for her famous chocolate-caramel whopper bars and she mixed up two batches. Your mom baked them at her place since there's no oven here. Didn't you know?"

He shrugged. "I've been trying to follow up on some leads in the evenings when Rain is sleeping, so I'm kind of out of touch." He raised an eyebrow at Vivienne. "Brownies for breakfast, Officer?"

Vivienne sniffed. "Life is short, Tyler. One must not turn down the blessed gift of a homemade dessert no matter when it's provided."

Penny laughed. "You are easily pleased, friend."

"Never underestimate the power contained in a sweet treat made with love. I'll get my pack. Be right back." She popped the rest of the brownie into her mouth and disappeared into the bathroom.

"Vivienne is a good roommate," Penny said fondly.

Tyler smiled at her. "It's nice to see you looking so happy."

She shrugged. "I love party planning. It's going to be so much fun to see everyone having a good time together. Your mom and Rain are coming, right?"

"Mom will bring Rain over and drop her off with us on her way to get a tooth fixed and come back after to join us. They'll be there at noon when it starts." He yawned again. "I should just about be awake by then."

"A shot of coffee and a couple of these brownies and you'll be doing wind sprints," Vivienne said, returning. She picked up a bag filled with party supplies and Penny and Tyler each carried a box. They paraded down to the back parking lot with the three dogs in tow. Tyler made them wait in the building while he checked the lot before he signaled to them to come out. Dusty and Scrappy sprawled contentedly in the back of Tyler's car and Penny took a spot in the passenger seat.

Vivienne slammed the trunk closed and loaded Hank into her own vehicle. After a thumbs-up, she drove out of the parking lot first. Tyler waited a few moments for her all-clear report before he followed.

"My mom must really like you if she's baking up your brownies."

"I think she would do that for anyone."

"She's not much of a baker. There was one cake episode I recall from my childhood that wound up with a fire-department response. I'm sure she was extra diligent with your treats. Somehow I think she'd do anything for you." He sighed.

"Because she's trying to set you up with a girlfriend?"

Now it was his turn to look chagrined. "It's her life mission to see me settled down. I told you before she feels responsible for how things ended with Diane.

She got some worrying signals while we were dating, but she never spoke up because I was head over heels for Diane and I probably wouldn't have listened, anyway. My dad was a powerful personality, and I think she learned how to keep her opinions to herself. We all did."

She cocked her head in his direction. "That must have been difficult."

He shrugged. "Dad was never comfortable showing emotions, except for disapproval. Mom was the nurturer and she was more patient than you can imagine with two boys. Since my brother is in the service, she's focused all her energies on me and Rain. I'm grateful for that. I don't know how I would manage the single-dad thing without her. Anyway, she's determined to right the sinking Walker ship for Rain's sake. I'm sorry if it's made you feel awkward."

"I think it's had that effect more on you than me."

"Maybe so. I've been gun-shy of relationships, so I have my radar up all the time." He frowned. "Except when I'm with you." His tone was puzzled.

"Should I be flattered or disappointed?"

He flicked a quick glance at her before his gaze returned to the road. "I'm not sure I'm much of a prize."

"Why would you say that?"

"Cop hours, single dad..." He hesitated. "Jaded older guy. Not the most attractive package."

"You love your daughter. There's nothing more attractive than that."

He shot her a sidelong glance. "Do you really think so?"

She felt suddenly uneasy, and laced her fingers in her lap. She'd just told the man he was attractive. Her nerves fluttered. "I wouldn't have said it if I hadn't meant it."

"I..." His eyes fixed on something in the rearview mirror, narrowing for a moment.

She could detect nothing but the normal New York traffic as they drove along, but his hands tightened on the wheel.

Her stomach knotted in an instant. “What?”

“Probably nothing. There’s a vehicle two car lengths back, a grey truck. Can’t see the driver. Could be purely innocent, but it’s been behind us for a bit now.”

Randall? Could he have gotten hold of another vehicle? Of course he could—he was capable of anything. She forced her fingers to loosen their death grip. In the side mirror she could barely see the truck. The memory surfaced of being locked in Randall’s trunk, hands bound and mouth taped, utterly helpless.

Not helpless, she told herself sharply. *You kicked out the taillight and helped Tyler find you.*

But if he hadn’t…

If he’d been a moment later…

She remembered the glint of the knife as Randall ran toward her. His green eyes had told her with absolute certainty that he intended to kill her.

She tried to push down the rising wave of panic. Cold sweat prickled her neck.

Tyler pulled down a side street. Her pulse hammered as she watched out the side mirror. The seconds ticked by, and the grey truck did not follow.

Tyler turned left and left again, circling back as traffic allowed. There was still no sign of the truck.

"Looks like we're clear." Tyler offered a reassuring smile. "I didn't mean to scare you."

The profound relief dizzied her. "Better safe than sorry."

"Right."

But she noticed that Tyler still did not appear quite as relaxed as he had before. Guilt rose alongside the relief. He was on edge and it was because she'd insisted on having the open house. She kept telling herself it was for the officers and their families, how disappointed they would be if the event was canceled. The reality was that Penny would be the most devastated of them all.

"Tyler, am I being selfish?" she blurted out.

He blinked at her. "About what?"

"Insisting on staying at work? Going forward with this party?" She looked out the window rather than at him. She could not bear to see condemnation. "The open house could have been postponed, or..." She swallowed. "It could have happened without me."

"No," he said, taking her hand. His hands were strong and warm. "It couldn't. No cop in the unit would consider canceling. It's important to you and you're important to all of us. You've helped make us a family, Penny."

She blushed. "You'd be a family without me."

"No. A family needs a rallying point, someone to remind them that relationships are the most important thing. You do that for us." He paused and his voice pitched lower. "You do that for me."

She knew her face was pink with pleasure. Was that what he really thought? Could she actually be the person he saw? A woman who helped glue their police family together? She went warm all over at his last words.

You do that for me.

But confusion seeped in through the pleasure. Did he mean friendship? Or did his heart beat with something much deeper, as she felt hers doing? She had no idea what to say.

"I know this is a bad time in your life, but after it's over, you'll be free to go after your goals. What do you want, Penny?"

"A family," she said instantly. "That's what I've always wanted."

His hand squeezed hers and he started to reply when his radio crackled and he released her.

Could she possibly be a part of Tyler's family one day? It made her breath catch to think of it. She wanted to mull over his words and hold them up to the autumn sunlight, examine them like the spectacularly colored fall leaves, but they'd pulled into a spot in front of headquarters and her musings would have to wait.

Hurrying inside, she plunged immediately into preparing the coffee and putting out the brownies. The treat quickly drew the early shift personnel, who seemed to share Vivienne's idea that brownies were a perfectly acceptable breakfast food. Everyone volunteered to help with the setup and she put them to work.

Her next job was decorating the conference room, and she firmly put out of her mind the horrible puppet box delivered to the police station. Nothing like that would happen again. Randall was not welcome in her thoughts. Today would be a celebration, a time to enjoy her police family. Tyler's earlier words came back to her.

A family needs a rallying point, someone

to remind them that relationships are the most important thing... You do that for me.

A little wisp of pleasure circled inside her as she covered the tables with festive fall cloths and added the tiny hay bales and smiling scarecrows. Jackson and Vivienne started prepping a lavish luncheon buffet in the kitchen so families would have plenty of choices. There would be everything from vegetarian lasagna to crispy fried lumpia. The dessert table was already crowded with pies and homemade fudge. Gavin's wife, Brianne, had brought two dozen of her famous caramel apples, spangled with sprinkles and chocolate chips. The pot of apple cider she'd set simmering on the stove would be the crowning autumn touch.

Another room was set up with activities for the kids. The pumpkin-cookie decorating station and dress-up clothes promised to be a hit with all the youngsters, especially Rain, she thought. And if all else failed, there was her surefire party pleaser—puppies.

Dr. Gina had already gated off a corner for a puppy play area and Brooke and her fuzzy babies were snoozing in an untidy pile of fat tummies and curvy tails. Gina had tied fall handkerchiefs around each animal's neck. Purely adorable, Penny thought. If that didn't make everyone stop and enjoy the party, nothing would.

Penny noted Gina gazing at the happy canines, a little crease between her eyebrows. She was probably wondering if Joel Carey would show up with proof that he owned the dog family, like he'd promised. Best not to dwell on that possibility at the moment.

The phone at her desk rang and she scurried to answer it. Technically, the office was not open for business matters on Saturday, but she was expecting a call from the local homeless shelter confirming that they would pick up all the leftover pumpkins to distribute to the children staying there.

"Brooklyn K-9 Unit," she said.

Silence.

"Hello? Is there anyone there?"

The connection ended. Her phone flashed the number from where the call had come. Local area code. Should she be worried? She no longer had the ability to distinguish worry from paranoia.

Henry called to her from the doorway. "Penny, where do you want this hay bale?"

"It's for the photo corner. I'll show you." After quickly texting Tyler about the hang-up call, she scurried back to the party plans.

"My guys are trying to get a location on that call," Caleb said. "Just in case it was Randall." Tyler found it disconcerting to talk to the FBI agent while he was dressed in overalls and a straw hat. Penny and Vivienne had talked him into being Farmer Black in the small pumpkin-patch area where the kids would be able to choose a pumpkin. "Beat cops are checking the area. No sign of Randall Gage."

"Could be unrelated," Tyler mused.

"Could be."

Lani appeared at his elbow. "Gavin pulled an extra unit to patrol the block until the party is over as a precaution."

Tyler relaxed a fraction. The building was secure. Even if it was Randall calling, he was not going to get anywhere near Penny, Bradley or anyone else. Still, he would keep his antenna on alert for the first sign of danger.

The office was buzzing with activity. A feeling of longing poked at him as he watched families arriving, moms and dads leading their excited children by the hand. Willow and Nate led Lucy in.

Tyler bent down to greet her. "Hello, Lucy. I'm so glad to see you. Rain will be here soon, and she'd love to play with you."

The child pressed her cheek into Willow's thigh.

"She's a little shy," Willow said.

"Totally fine." The girl had a right to be withdrawn. He saw in her what Penny might have been like as a child. Already the victim of neglect and then to become an orphan after witnessing her parents' execution? At least Lucy had an amazing couple to adopt her, as Penny had. He watched the threesome walk by. Nate hoisted Lucy up on his shoulders. Her squeak of laughter penetrated the party noise. A perfect family, he thought.

Why did he keep picturing himself and Penny squiring Rain around the festivities? Since Diane had left, he'd written his single-dad identity in stone, but something was chipping away at that stone at an ever increasing rate. A certain red-haired, freckle-faced, tenderhearted woman. She wanted an intact family, and so did he. She loved Rain, like he did.

But the rules…the solid reasons he'd pondered why dating Penny was a bad idea.

He blinked. "I need coffee," he said aloud. He'd turned in that direction as his mother arrived with Rain in tow. Thanks to Grandma, Rain's yellow pants and sweater actually matched and her hair was neatly contained in two curly pigtails. He was getting to be pretty masterful at wrestling her curly mop under the control of a half-dozen barrettes, but he was a long way from conquering pigtails. Babby was clutched under Rain's arm. She immediately reached for him. "Daddy."

Francine handed her over. "Be good, baby. See you soon."

Daddy. How he relished hearing that word. Someday she would look around and wonder why she didn't have a mommy like the other kids. That thought struck him hard until he reminded himself that for the moment Rain wanted him, adored him, favored him out of all other people in the world. That made his heart swell, until Penny walked in and Rain immediately stuck out her arms in her direction.

"Enny," she said.

Penny laughed and Tyler handed over his daughter, mildly offended and thrilled at the same time. It was clear that Rain adored Penny. That thought made his nerves tumble. His daughter was not afraid to open her heart fully to this woman. Should he follow suit? Embrace the images his imagination supplied of the three of them together, enjoying life? But what about his list of excellent reasons to shy away? And what if down the road Penny decided she did not love him enough to stay, just as Diane had concluded? His skin went cold.

"Earth to Tyler."

He jerked from his thoughts as Caleb shoved a large cardboard carton at him. "Congratulations, Detective, you've been nominated to go lug the other box of pumpkins from the storage room and bring them here."

Tyler chuckled. "I have? Why don't you do it? You're the big burly farmer."

"I know, and my muscles are way bigger than yours, but I'm busy pulling weeds and keeping the crows out of my pumpkin patch and that's a full-time job. Hop to it, Walker. The kids are waiting."

Tyler saluted. "Yes, sir, Farmer Black." He turned to Penny. "Is it okay if Rain stays with you for a while?"

"Of course. I'll help her decorate a cookie." She snuggled Rain close, and Tyler noted how his daughter relaxed in her embrace, cheek pressed close to Penny's. Two peas in a pod, his mother would say.

Best not to think about that. In the storage room, he located the box of pumpkins and hauled it where he'd been directed. He, Caleb and Vivienne laid them out in the pretend pumpkin patch to the delight of the waiting children. Caleb, grinning from ear to ear, took his spot next to a bale of hay.

"All right, children," he announced in a booming voice. "Who would like to pick out one of my prize-winning pumpkins to take home? You won't find a finer set of pumpkins anywhere, I guarantee. Best pumpkins in the whole state of New York, maybe even the world." There was a chorus of excited voices and several children trotted happily into the patch.

Vivienne eyed her husband adoringly. "He's really getting into the role, isn't he? I even saw him looking at tractors online."

"Watch out or you'll be trading in your badge for a pitchfork," Tyler warned.

She laughed. "If that's where life takes us, I'm in. Police work or pumpkins. As long as we're together, we can do anything."

He felt the swell of longing again as he watched Vivienne join Caleb and press a kiss to his cheek. Tyler searched for Penny and Rain.

He spotted Penny at the decorating table, helping Rain select a sugar cookie from the pile. Of course, his daughter had picked the one on the bottom, so Penny was delicately rearranging the tower of treats to accommodate.

His cell phone buzzed with a text from Bradley. Call me. His heart ticked up a notch. He caught Penny's eye, gesturing with his cell phone that he needed to make a call. When she nodded, he stepped out and went to his cubicle. Dusty followed along.

"Need some quiet time, girl?"

Dusty crawled into her crate near his desk and flopped down for a snooze while he dialed Bradley's number.

"You're missing a good party," Tyler said.

"I know. I'm on my way. Figured I'd call from the car but you didn't pick up."

"Sorry, I was hauling pumpkins. What did you get?"

"Remember the lead on someone named Andy, who was house-sitting for someone on the Emerys' street around the time of the murders? I finally tracked that Andy down."

Tyler's stomach tightened. Young Lucy Emery had told them her favorite person besides her Aunt Willow and Uncle Nate was someone named Andy, someone with brown hair. It was their only slim lead on a possible witness to who had killed the Emerys. Perhaps the "Andy" clue referred to the killer himself, someone bent on delivering Lucy from the care of her neglectful parents. Maybe Randall, maybe not. He held the phone tight. "Did you find him?"

"Yes and no."

He groaned. "You're killing me. Spit it out, Bradley."

"Yes, I found one Andy Spinoza, who was house-sitting six doors down at the time of the murder." He paused. "Andy is short for Andrea."

He blinked. "A woman?"

"Yep."

Lucy had been adamant that Andy was

a male, but she might have been mistaken.

Tyler sat forward. "Does she have brown hair at least?"

"Nope. She's seventy-two and her hair is white as the driven snow. What's more, she claimed she'd never met Lucy Emery or her parents."

"Is she telling the truth?"

"Yeah. Her details check out."

Tyler had to restrain himself from not thunking his head on the desktop. "Another dead end."

"That's an affirmative. I'll be back at the office in ten."

"Copy that."

He pushed back his chair, slapping his thighs in frustration. He was becoming more and more convinced that the whole Andy thing was simple confusion or imagination from the mind of a traumatized child. At the moment, it was a lead that went nowhere in answering the question that burned in all their minds.

Was Randall Gage the Emerys' killer, too?

That's the number-two priority, he reminded himself.

His first mission was to capture Randall and lock him in a cell.

Permanently.

The murmur of party noise drifted down the halls, but suddenly he did not feel in a festive mood. The open house was a momentary distraction, but the danger remained undiminished. As soon as the party ended, he would redouble his efforts and beat the bushes for any meager clue that might lead him to his quarry.

With so many cops looking for him, Randall was living on borrowed time.

And that meant Penny was, too.

THIRTEEN

Penny helped Rain spread orange frosting on her pumpkin cookie. She held up the tray of decorations. “What do you want to put on your pretty pumpkin?” Rain scooped up a collection of goodies with her plastic spoon and festooned her treat entirely with orange candies and sprinkles. She refused any other colored item.

“Well, that’s orange all right,” Penny said with a smile. “Your daddy will like it.” She glanced around but Tyler had not returned. She wondered if the call had anything to do with Bradley’s absence. Her nerves tightened. She wished her brother would arrive soon. The longer he was away, the more her worry mounted. What if Randall changed his mind and decided to harm Bradley first? Her throat went dry.

"See?"

Penny refocused on Rain, who was holding up her cookie for Penny to admire. "What a great job you did."

"Daddy?" Rain said.

"He'll be back in minute. Are you going to share your cookie with him?"

Rain immediately shoved in a big bite that puffed out her cheeks.

Penny giggled. "Every good chef has to taste-test first, I guess."

Rain put down the cookie and climbed off the chair in search of the puppies. "Hold on there, sticky girl," Penny said, snagging Rain's gummy hand. "We have to wash first. Then you can see the puppies."

Rain complained. "Doggies."

"Frosting is bad for doggies," Penny insisted. "And besides we have some fun foamy soap in the ladies' room."

Relenting, Rain clutched Babby under

her armpit and followed Penny into the ladies' room. Penny turned on the water and got the temperature adjusted correctly, but Rain was too short to reach. There was a stool in the tiny corner cabinet, where the other desk clerk stored extra sets of clothes for her one-year-old twin girls. "Hold your hands up for a second, Rain, while I get the stool. Like this." Penny demonstrated.

The little girl thrust her own sticky hands up high.

"Stay right there for just one minute."

Penny went to the corner and opened the cabinet door. She had to get on her knees to reach the stool. "Okay. Got it. Step up on..." Her heart jolted as she turned around. Rain was not there.

Immediately, Penny pushed open the two stall doors. "Rain?"

There was no sign of her. Whirling, she ran to the door. When she saw a sticky orange handprint indicating the child had exited, she went cold all over. Stomach clenched, Penny ran out into the hallway. Babby was lying on the floor and she snatched it up. "Rain?" she called. Scrappy must have heard her from where he was playing in the puppy area. He came bounding up quickly and skidded to a stop.

Vivienne appeared, carrying a roll of paper towels.

"What's up, Penny?"

"Rain's wandered off."

Vivienne frowned. "She couldn't have gone far. I'll check the kitchen."

"I'll go to the kid area." Penny sprinted down the hall. Surely that must be what had happened. Rain couldn't wait to have her hands washed. She'd gone on her own to find the puppies. Bursting into the room, she scanned the crowd. There were kids picking up pumpkins and others trying on tutus and cowboy boots. Three were busily absorbed in creating cookie masterpieces. None of them was Rain. The knot in her stomach tightened.

She whirled and ran out, plowing into Tyler in the doorway.

"What's wrong?"

"Rain."

His blue eyes darkened to steel. He clenched her forearm. "What happened?"

"I was washing her hands in the bathroom. I turned to get the stool and she disappeared."

His tone went flat and hard. "Where have you looked?"

"The hallway and here. I just…"

Vivienne poked her head in. "Rain's not in the kitchen. Jackson said she wasn't in the stairwell, either."

Tyler and Penny both sprinted to the larger conference room. Families were chatting away and eating platefuls of food. Gavin looked up from his bite of pasta, his eyes narrowing.

"Walker?"

"Rain's missing."

He immediately put down his fork and pushed back from the table.

Bradley was just sitting down with a plate of sliced brisket and potato salad in the spot next to Gavin. He bolted from his chair with King. "We'll search the parking lot, just in case she got outside the building. Seal it off. I'll check with the patrol cop."

"What should I do?" Penny almost sobbed.

"Nothing," Tyler snapped.

It was hard to breathe. "I could check outside, make sure—"

"No. I'll handle this." His expression turned to granite as he took Rain's bunny from her clutched fingers. "Stay here. I'm going to get Dusty." He ran toward his cubicle, returning in a moment with Dusty. Penny could only look on with her heart in her throat as the recrimination pounded her.

She had lost Tyler's daughter.

She looked up to find Willow touching her arm. "It's okay. They'll find her." Lucy was tucked in her other arm. So small, so dependent on her adopted mother. Rain had trusted Penny to care for her.

And Tyler had trusted Penny, too.

She choked back a sob as all around her cops began to search every square inch of the building. Tyler thrust Rain's bunny at Dusty. "Track, girl."

Dusty trotted down the hallway, nose glued to the floor. Penny followed Tyler on shaky legs. His back was rigid with tension. A million thoughts ran through Penny's brain. If Rain had gotten out somehow, wandered into the street… If Randall was watching the building…had lured her away.

She remembered what Randall had said about her parents. They were neglectful, bad parents. Was she bad, too?

Was that what she was destined to be? A bad mother? She slowed to dash the tears from her eyes. Vivienne raced down the stairwell. "She's not upstairs."

Visions swirled through Penny's head, each more far-fetched and terrible than the last. Rain hit by a car. Tumbling out an open window. Vanished, never to be recovered again.

The panic made her feel light-headed.

Vivienne reached out a hand. "Maybe you should sit down here for a minute."

She leaned against the wall to steady herself and prayed with all her might that Rain would be found. From the direction of the front office, she heard a shout.

"She's in here. I found her," Tyler yelled.

Found her. Hurt? Or worse?

Penny's knees went weak, but she forced herself to continue into the reception area. She peered at the cops gathered around, then edged past them with nerves quaking. Rain was there, curled up underneath Penny's desk on Scrappy's cushion. Tyler tossed a rope toy to reward Dusty, then sank to his knees next to his daughter.

Penny leaned on the door for support, her vision blurred with unshed tears. *Thank You, God.* Her heart quivered with gratitude and pain. Tyler had trusted her with his most precious possession and she'd let him down, let Rain down.

"That was very naughty," Tyler said to Rain. "You should have stayed where Miss Penny told you and not left the bathroom."

Rain pulled a frown and stuck her sticky thumb into her mouth. She would not look her father in the eye.

"Daddy and Miss Penny were worried about you," he continued. "All the officers were looking everywhere. They were all feeling scared and sad because you were gone. I felt scared, too." Rain started to whimper, and Tyler pulled her into his arms, sticky hands and all. He stood with the child clinging to him. He leaned his face against her pigtails and Penny read in the lines of his posture the utter relief as the terror ebbed away. In a moment, he would turn around to face her.

She did not want to see the look in his eyes, the expression that revealed his disappointment in her, the woman who'd lost his daughter.

She'd neglected Rain, lost her, put her at risk.

Before he could say a word, she hurried out of the room.

Tyler kept his expression stern as he cleaned Rain's palms with a wet wipe. His pulse was still elevated, and the harsh tone he'd used when he'd barked orders at Penny rang in his mind. He hadn't faulted her for letting Rain slip away, not really. It had happened to him, too, and the sheer panic that erupted when it had happened pushed him into cop mode both times. Now he looked around for Penny as the partygoers relaxed back into the festivities. The expression on her face when she'd told him Rain was missing had been nothing short of unadulterated terror. He had to find her, had to apologize.

Tyler toted Rain and her bunny, determined not to take his eyes off his precocious daughter as he searched.

Ten minutes later, his mom arrived, and he'd still not found Penny.

"What's wrong?" she said. "You're worried about something, I can tell. What happened?"

"Nothing. Just a small glitch. Penny was watching Rain and she wandered off. That's all."

Francine frowned. "You didn't yell at Penny, did you?"

"No." He paused, grimacing. "Not exactly yelled."

She skewered him with a look. "As in 'not exactly but I used that horrible I'm-in-charge tone' that crops up whenever you feel like things are out of control?"

He huffed out a breath. "Probably."

"Probably?"

"Okay, I did use that tone, but I'm going to apologize as soon as I can. I've been looking all over for her."

Francine took Rain. "An excellent idea.

Go find her right away and tell her your behavior was inexcusable and you're very, very sorry. It wouldn't hurt to order her some flowers later, too. Roses would be nice. I'm taking this kiddo straight to the bathroom for a good hand-washing. Get busy, Ty."

"Yes, ma'am," he said meekly. Bradley. He would know where his sister was. But Bradley was absent from the dining table.

"He went to the break room, I think," Vivienne told him.

Bradley was indeed in the break room, staring into a cup of coffee, his plate of uneaten food nearby. Penelope was not with him.

"Where's Penny?"

Bradley studied him coldly. "She needs some time alone," he said.

"No, that's not what she needs. She needs an apology from this blockhead for snapping at her."

Bradley didn't smile but his expression relaxed slightly. "If you were any other guy, I'd be reaming you out for hurting her feelings, but I know this is more about her than you."

He sank down in a chair across from Bradley. "How so?"

"Her deepest fear is that she is going to be like our mom and dad and she'll let her own kids down. That's why she breaks off relationships, I think. She's afraid to find out she's cut from the same cloth they were."

"That's nonsense. She's the most loving person I know."

"Yeah," he said with a thoughtful look at Tyler. "And she cares a lot about you and Rain. She's allowed herself to get close to you both, I've noticed. It required a lot of courage on her part." There was an accusation in his tone.

Tyler rolled his shoulders, suddenly weary. "And I shook her confidence, didn't I?"

"Probably, but I'm sure you can apologize sufficiently and she'll understand."

He paused. "What I'm more concerned about is what happens from here."

"What do you mean?"

"If history is any indication, my guess is she's going to distance herself from you both."

A sharp pain cut at him.

"Is that what you want?" Bradley asked.

"Me?" Was that what he wanted? A simple way out of his emotional dilemma? It would be so much easier than having to deal with his untidy heap of emotions. "No," he said after a minute. "I care about your sister."

Bradley folded his arms. "That's what I thought. And she cares about you, too, so if you want her in your life, let me give you a word of advice. Don't let her walk away because she won't come back. If you do convince her to stay, you'd better mean it for the long term." Bradley stood. "That's all I've got to say. I'm going to go finish my lunch."

"Where is she, Bradley? I have to talk to her."

"She doesn't want me to tell you, but you know my sister." He offered an innocent shrug. "She's a hard worker. Any excuse to tidy up the files…" He let the words drift away.

Files. Tyler made a beeline for the small file room close to the front office.

Penny was there leaning against a cabinet, arms hugging herself. Scrappy hovered nearby. Her face was blotched from crying. When she saw him, she gulped and straightened. "I was just… I mean… I had a file to return so I figured…"

He stepped close. "Penny, listen to me. I am so sorry. My tone with you was unnecessary. I absolutely don't blame you for losing track of Rain. She's a crafty one, for sure." He tried a smile, which she did not return.

"Perfectly okay," she said brightly. "I never should have turned my back on her.

I probably shouldn't have thought I could take care of her in the first place."

"No, really, Penny. I get it. It's happened to me. It wasn't your fault and you didn't do anything wrong or neglectful."

The word seemed to slap at her. She jerked back as if to keep the maximum distance between them. "That's nice of you to say. Thank you. I need to get back to the party."

He reached out a hand. "No, please, Penny. Listen to me. I…"

The phone rang in the outer office. "I'd better get that. Waiting on a call from the homeless shelter."

"Penny…"

But she'd skirted around him and darted into the outer office. He followed.

Whatever damage he'd caused, he had to show her that the fault had been his and his entirely.

If he didn't succeed, he had a feeling she would drift right out of his life for good.

FOURTEEN

The phone at her desk rang a third time before she got there. She wanted to grab her purse and head right out the door, but she could not leave the open house, not until everything was cleaned up and the last guest had left. At least if she could tackle the phone call, maybe Tyler would leave and she could regain her composure.

She sucked in a breath and steadied herself as the phone rang again. Work would restore her purpose. Work would salve the raw place in her soul, the place that said, "You'd be a bad mom, just like your own mother was."

She grabbed the phone. "Brooklyn K-9 Unit, how may I help you?"

"Hello, Penny," Randall said. "Why didn't I get an invitation to the party?"

Ice flashed across her nerves, freezing her an inch at a time. Tyler must have read the shock in her posture. He ran to her side and hit the speakerphone button.

"Who is this?" he demanded.

"Hello, Detective Walker. I'd recognize your voice anywhere. This is the guy you shot at the docks. My side's still killing me, by the way."

Penny realized she was still holding the receiver and she set it softly down on the cradle, fingers shaking. "What do you want?"

"Lots of things, but I'm not going to get any of them. The cops have done an excellent job sealing off the area. There's nowhere for me to go, not even to my apartment. So what's left for me? You know the answer to that, Penny. Only one thing, or two, to be specific."

Tyler leaned close to the phone. "You're

not going to get it," he growled. "Give yourself up. You'll get a fair trial at least."

"Not likely, when you are all busily trying to frame me for the Emery murders, too."

"Same clown mask, same MO. Give us something to prove it wasn't you."

There was a pause. "What do I get in exchange for doing your work for you?"

"What do you want?" Tyler asked.

"A get-out-of-jail-free pass."

Tyler grimaced. "Not possible, but going to jail for one set of murders is preferable to two sets, isn't it?"

"Okay, how about I tell you I wasn't even in the area when those two got offed?"

"Got an alibi to that effect?"

Bradley and King hurried in. Penny put a finger to her lips.

"I was visiting a lady friend in the Catskills the night the Emerys were killed. I was there a few days. You know I go up there sometimes—it's where I conked your fancy-pants FBI agent on the head and knocked him out back in July, remember?"

"It's all about timing," Tyler said. "You could have killed the Emerys before you fled there in April."

"My bus ticket proves I wasn't anywhere near the Emery home when they were shot."

"Anyone can buy a bus ticket."

"Don't treat me like an idiot. Bus stations got video. Do your job and find yourself another killer. It's enough for me to get rid of the McGregor family. The parents deserved to die. How many times did I see the kids wandering the streets while their worthless parents were out getting drunk? Whoever killed the Emerys might have noticed that kid being ignored, too. Maybe you should be thanking that copycat killer for getting rid of a couple of losers who didn't deserve a kid, anyway."

Penny swallowed convulsively. She thought of her parents, the woman who kissed her ouchies and the father who would play his harmonica from time to time. They didn't deserve to be murdered.

"That wasn't your decision to make," Tyler said.

Randall snorted. "Well, I made it, anyway, didn't I? So what do I get for all that information?"

"You get nothing except a trip to jail," Bradley snarled.

Randall laughed. "Is that you, Bradley? Sorry, kid. You have to wait your turn until I take care of your sister."

Bradley looked as though he was going to snatch the phone up and break it in half.

"Did you like the puppet, Penny? I made it just for you. Figure I'm going to be seeing you real soon."

Tyler's chin jutted out. "Why don't you meet me face-to-face? You got a problem with the McGregors? Tell me all about it in person."

"I am not interested in you, Detective. I made a promise and Penny knows that I keep my promises, don't you?"

She swallowed. Her voice came out in a whisper. "You're never going to stop, are you?"

"Not until you and your brother are dead. I'll have that to keep me warm at night when they put me away." He laughed again. "You know what they say. In for a Penny, in for a pound. See you soon."

The connection ended.

There was a sound of breaking glass from outside. Tyler pulled Penny down below the counter. "Stay low."

He ran out the front door, Bradley right behind him with King.

Her body went numb with fear. Randall was out there, watching. She'd been a fool to think all the protection they'd put in place would dissuade him. All of her family, her police family, including Rain and the children, had been put at risk because of her. She had been selfish, she realized, and there was only one course of action to take.

But first, she pressed her hands together

and prayed for the safety of Tyler and her brother. Minutes ticked by and there was a buzz of movement, radios and cell phones going off as word spread through the open house.

Tyler and Bradley returned. Bradley was carrying King. Penny's heart dropped.

"Get me some paper towels," Bradley called, holding King's paw. Horrified, she saw red dripping onto the entry tile. Vivienne rushed over with a roll of towels. "I'll get Dr. Gina."

"He doesn't need a vet, it's paint. Randall threw a glass jar full of it at Tyler's vehicle. That was followed by a rock with a bus-ticket stub attached. King stepped in the paint splatter before I could stop him but I managed to keep him away from the glass shards."

Tyler grunted. "Cop out front said Randall was in a grey truck. He took off. They're trying to track him." He held King's leash while Bradley wiped off the paint.

"You're okay, boy," Bradley said to King. "He needs a bath before he starts licking his paws. Let me hose him off and I'll get Caleb. We'll help with the search."

"I'll go now, too." Tyler looked at Caleb. "Call me when the scene's processed and I'll start chasing down that bus-ticket information."

Before he headed for the door, Tyler's eyes found hers. Randall was close, and he'd singled out Tyler's car. The target had widened from Penny and Bradley to Tyler, too.

There was only one decision left for her to make.

It wasn't until hours later that she went in search of Gavin, pain impossibly heavy in her heart.

She found him behind his desk, peering at his computer screen. His phone rang and he gestured her into a seat as he picked it up.

"No, the police department has no statement at this time other than what you got from our public information officer." He hung up the phone. It rang again and he let it go to voice mail.

"Sorry. It's been ringing pretty steadily. I don't know how the media gets hold of details almost as soon as they happen. They are all circling like sharks, hoping to dig up some headlines." He folded his hands. "How are you doing? It's been an eventful day."

She nodded, her throat closing up.

"The party was a success," he said gently. "In spite of…everything."

She sucked in a steadying breath. "That's why I'm here. I wanted to have this party so badly, I didn't consider that I would be putting people at risk."

"Randall didn't hurt anyone."

"But he could have. He got close enough to throw paint. He might have been shooting instead."

Gavin listened intently. "Penny, we are going to get Randall Gage. It's a matter of time, but if you need some days off to ease your mind then—"

"I'm going to resign."

He raised both eyebrows. "That's not necessary."

"Yes, it is." She explained the details of her plan.

"Take a leave of absence instead. Let things settle."

"And you'll keep me in a secure room at the hotel until they do? For weeks? Months? Randall's been at large for more than two decades already. My brother and Tyler can't get anything done while they are watching me around the clock."

"Penny..."

She got up. "I don't want to leave, Sarge. This is my home. I..." She swallowed hard. "It's what I need to do."

She did not wait for his reply as she scurried out the door.

On Monday morning, the cops were all laser-focused on Tyler as he readied his report. He felt conflicted about what he had to tell them.

"Randall's alibis for the Emery murders check out. The bus driver remembers him and there's video footage of him getting on the bus the day before. He was on his way to a friend's place who let him stay. Convenience-store clerk in Monticello also has footage of Randall buying cigarettes the evening of the murder."

Gavin exhaled. "So it's certain then. We've got ourselves a copycat murderer."

Nate Slater had gone pale. "Lucy could still be a target."

"We'll get them," Gavin said. "Similar motives perhaps. We're looking for someone who knew firsthand how Lucy was being neglected by her parents, so it was someone with easy access to the situation."

Tyler winced, thinking about Penny. He'd tried to see her on Sunday, but Vivienne said she was in bed with a headache.

His calls had gone unreturned, along with his texts.

Jackson drummed his fingers on the table. "We've discussed that neglect motive. We'll move forward with that line of thinking now that we've ruled Randall out."

An office clerk popped her head in. "Bradley, reporter on the phone for you, looking for an interview. Her name's Sasha Eastman."

Bradley grimaced. "Tell her thanks, but no thanks."

The clerk nodded and left.

Gavin stood. "There's another announcement."

Tyler noticed that Bradley's gaze was cemented to the tabletop. Whatever it was, he already knew about it. An alarm bell began to jingle way down in Tyler's gut.

Gavin blew out a breath. "Penny has given her notice."

"What?" Tyler said. He almost leaped to his feet.

"I told her she can use her vacation days for her two weeks as long as she comes in for a little gathering so we can say goodbye properly. She feels that she is drawing unwanted attention from the public, which is distracting from our work and possibly jeopardizing our safety here at the station, and that of her brother, by continuing to work here."

"That's not—"

Gavin stopped Tyler with a look. "I don't want her to go any more than you do, but the fact is, Randall's gotten close, too close, too many times."

"For how long? Until Randall's caught?"

Gavin's mouth twitched. "She's seeking a position with a K-9 unit in the Bronx, pending our capture of Randall. She's asked me for a recommendation, and I've provided her with one. If she is hired, I would imagine she will not be returning to her employment here."

Tyler sat back in his chair. Disbelief circled inside him, along with sorrow and anger. So she was leaving him, too, just like Diane, without a backward glance for him or Rain. Abruptly he got up and left the conference room, stalking toward his cubicle.

Bradley caught up with him. "If it means anything, she doesn't want to leave."

"Then she shouldn't," he snapped. "Or at the very least she could have talked about it with me."

His eyes narrowed. "Maybe she thought you'd get angry just like you are now."

"Don't I have a right to be?"

"I don't know," Bradley said. "Do you?"

"What are you saying?"

Bradley folded his arms across his chest. "What does she mean to you?"

Tyler stopped, mouth open. *Everything.* For some reason the thought stripped him of the power of speech. He stood there, gaping and mute.

"You said you wanted her around and I told you she would bolt if you didn't give her reason not to. What reassurances have you given her, Tyler?" Bradley let the silence go on for a moment. "Penny is more sensitive than most women and there are plenty of legit circumstances that made her that way. If you haven't given her any clear indication of how you feel about her, then like I said, she's got no reason to stay."

"I tried… I mean…" What had he given her? The vague sentiments about wanting to date her, spend time with her after Randall's capture? Nothing concrete—he hadn't had the spine. His mouth snapped shut.

Bradley's lips thinned into a tight line. "She's giving up everything she loves because it's best for everyone else. Don't make it harder on her, Tyler. If you're not willing to risk a relationship, then back off. She doesn't deserve any more pain."

Tyler watched Bradley go. What was happening? Why was his world turning upside down again? Why did he feel as though his heart was being yanked from his body in one quivering chunk?

He knew two things. First, he had to talk to Penny. But more than that, he needed to figure out the answer to Bradley's question.

What does Penny mean to you?

FIFTEEN

Palms sweating, he knocked on the door of the hotel safe room. Vivienne answered. "Glad you're here. I need to go take Hank out for some exercise. He's climbing the walls."

Though he wanted to tell her she didn't need to leave, he was secretly relieved she was stepping out. He had no idea how the conversation with Penny would go, but it would be harder with a third party in the room. She hastily departed. After a fortifying breath, he stepped inside.

Penny was folding clothes and stowing them in a pile resting next to her on the sofa. Her hair was caught in a soft ponytail. "Hello, Tyler." She did not look at him after her polite greeting.

"Hi. I heard from Gavin that you were quitting."

She seemed to curl in a bit on herself. "Yes."

"And looking for another position?" He hadn't meant for it to be such an abrupt statement, but it came out that way nonetheless.

"As soon as Randall is caught," she said. "It's for the best."

"Why? If he's caught, you'll be safe. No more threats to you or Bradley."

She sighed. "I need a fresh start, Tyler."

"Why didn't you talk to me about it?"

She stopped and shot him a quick glance. "I needed to think with my head, not with my heart."

He blinked. "But we can still see each other, even if you don't work in Brooklyn, right?"

Her long pause told him everything. She wasn't just leaving her job, she was walking away from him. He heaved out the breath he hadn't realized he was holding. "I see."

"I don't want to go, but I have to. I—I will be sad to leave you and Rain. I care about you both."

"And we care about you, too. I'm sorry if I was too scared to lay it out clearly, but—"

"I can't," she said, tears glistening. "I can't stay and risk hurting you or Rain."

"You won't."

"I have a murderer tracking me who will never give up. And even if I didn't..."

"What? What is it? Say it." He felt a growing desperation.

"I'm not sure I will ever be confident enough to be a fixture in Rain's life and I would never be able to stand it if I let her down."

"Penny..." He tried to grab her hand, but she pulled away. "You wouldn't do that."

"You can't know that. I'm doing what's best."

"So you're going to leave us." He fisted his hands on his hips. "Without a word."

"I didn't want to make matters worse."

"And you were afraid I'd try and talk you out of it." He shook his head. "You should have talked to me. You're leaving just like..." He broke off, his insides burning as if he'd swallowed poison.

Now she turned her chocolate gaze on him. "I think you mean 'just like Diane did.'"

He sucked in a breath. "This has nothing to do with my ex-wife."

"You're right. It doesn't. And this isn't about you or Rain or how I feel about you both."

He could not contain the bitter laugh. "Believe it or not, that's exactly what Diane said before she dumped us like last week's trash."

Penny winced. "I'm very sorry."

"She was sorry, too, but not sorry enough to stay."

Her eyes flashed with emotion. "Don't

lump me with your ex-wife. I am not Diane."

Hurt, betrayal and, most of all, a terrible sense of failure enveloped him. "You might as well be."

She flushed red. "That is totally unfair."

"I'm a single father and I shouldn't have let you become a part of our lives. I should have known you were going to leave us." His voice almost broke on the last word.

"Tyler..." Her shock hung in the air. "I didn't..."

His hurt came from a deep-down place because he now knew the answer to Bradley's question. What did she mean to him? She meant everything and now she was leaving him, leaving them. The pain tore at him until he could almost not get a breath. It was his own fault. He hadn't done enough for her to want to stay.

"Please..." she said, but he turned to go.

I want you to stay. I want to love you, and make a life with you and Rain. He wanted so many things, but now he knew their ending would be just like it had been with Diane.

"I hope you'll be happy in the Bronx, Penny." Then he escaped, practically running from the room as fast as he could go.

In his car, he rested his head on the steering wheel. What had he just done? How in the space of a few minutes had it all fallen apart? He wanted to get in his car and drive away somewhere quiet, where he could think, but his mom was waiting for him to pick up Rain. *You're a father. That's what's left for you, Tyler, nothing more.* Heart heavy as a stone, he returned home.

His mother looked up from her crocheting when he entered the apartment. "What's wrong?"

He sank on the sofa with a groan. "Where's Rain?"

"Napping. Tell me what happened."

He didn't bother wondering how she knew. "Penny's quitting."

Her fingers stilled on the crochet hooks. "For good?"

"Seems that way. And she's going to get another job, move on to another life." He closed his eyes. "I can't believe this is happening again. I cared about her, I really did."

"Do."

He opened his eyes. "It's over, Mom. You can't make someone stay. I learned that the hard way."

"Did you ask her to stay?"

He felt a rise of irritation. "I'm not going to beg, Mom. It was enough to do that with Diane."

She stabbed the hooks into her ball of yarn. "Tyler William Walker, you listen to me and you listen well."

He sat up straighter.

"Penny is not Diane. What's more, you are not the same man you were two years ago."

"I know that."

"Do you?" Her eyes blazed at him. "Because from where I'm sitting, you are so busy looking back that you're losing a treasure right in front of you."

"You're beginning to sound like Bradley."

"I always knew that young man was smart." She picked up her yarn ball and purse. "You know what? I didn't speak up to your father as much as I should have because I didn't want to make waves. And I didn't express my misgivings about Diane for the same reason. Well, I'm speaking up now, Ty. Stop looking behind you. God gave you two eyes in the front of your head, not the back, for a reason." And with that, she walked to the apartment door and slammed it behind her, leaving him gaping.

What was he supposed to do next? The apartment settled into quiet. He lied down on the couch, his mind alive with snippets of conversation.

What does she mean to you?

Stop looking behind you.

I care for you both.

He closed his eyes and folded his hands. The most important conversation he needed to have at this moment was between him and the Lord.

Penny fought against tears as she carefully loaded the personal effects from her desk into a cardboard box the next morning. The photo of her adoptive parents and her brother on the day he'd earned his badge made her pause. She'd nearly burst with pride at that moment. The second photo was one of her standing next to him in her uniform shirt. It had seemed on that day that maybe she had finally restarted her life on a path that would lead her into the future, away from the sadness and tragedy that had defined her past.

That had all come to a violent end when Randall had shown up. Everything was crumbling around her. The biggest blow was having to leave her police family.

And Tyler…

His image came uninvited into her thoughts. She'd been trying valiantly to forget his harsh condemnation.

I should have known you were going to leave us. It was all so shocking. She hadn't known there was an *us* except in her imagination. Worse than the words, worse than any of it, had been the catch in his voice when he'd said it.

He'd painted her with the same brush as Diane…as an immature woman who'd walked out on him and Rain. She didn't know what to do, how to fix it, except to leave the whole situation behind. Was she being cowardly or kind? She had no idea.

She was jotting down notes to discuss with the person who would be taking over her job, when Joel Carey, the man who insisted Brooke and her pups belonged to him, came through the door. Since her replacement was grabbing a cup of coffee, she plastered on a polite smile.

"How can I help you, sir?"

He waved a photo triumphantly and

slapped it on the counter. "I'm here to claim my dogs. Take a look."

She peered at the grainy photo of Carey standing next to a German shepherd. He was not smiling in the picture. The dog was a beautiful specimen, as far as she could tell.

"See? The dog's mine and so are her puppies. I want them now."

"One moment, please." With a sinking stomach, Penny quickly summoned Gavin and Dr. Gina, who were settling some paperwork in the back room. They both arrived on the double.

Carey waved the photo around and Gavin and Gina examined it.

"It's a little blurry," Gina said. "That could be any dog. It doesn't have to be Brooke."

Carey's eyes narrowed. "Rory is her name and it's not just the photo. That homeless guy told you he remembered me calling to her, trying to get her back, but the traffic was too bad. And you promised that if I brought proof, the dogs would be turned over. Here's the proof. Are you reneging on your word?"

Gavin blew out a breath, his eyebrows knitted together. "No, you've produced the photo and we will release the dogs to you."

Gina went stiff and Penny could see the anguish in her face, but she did not contradict Sarge.

Carey gave a satisfied nod. "Let me have 'em."

"Not right now," Gavin said. "I'm sure Dr. Gina needs to wrap up a few things before she releases them."

Carey fisted his hands on his hips and glowered.

Gina nodded. "I'll need to keep them for a few days. They need their next round of shots."

"No way…" Carey began.

Sarge stared him down. "You want what's best for these pups, don't you, Mr. Carey? You wouldn't want to compromise their care in any way, after you've worked so hard to get them back."

Carey squirmed. "All right. I'll be here next week on Monday morning to pick them up." He smiled. "Take good care of my dogs," he called before he left.

Gina sagged as the door closed. "He's just going to sell them. I can feel it. He doesn't love these dogs. That photo might be another dog entirely."

"I'm sorry, Gina, truly I am," Sarge said, "but we have no grounds to keep them from him any longer."

He touched Gina's shoulder and walked back to his office.

Penny went to Gina and hugged her. Gina sniffled against the tears. "I guess I knew it would come to this, but I hate the thought of turning them over to a guy like that. I was hoping he'd give up and leave them with us."

"You've taken such wonderful care of Brooke and her babies." Penny squeezed her and let her go to hand her a tissue.

"Everybody will be crushed around here," she said. *Especially a little curly-haired tyke named Rain.*

She remembered Rain's squeals of delight as she tumbled and played with the pups, and the tender moment when she'd been able to soothe the child's hurt fingers.

How would Tyler explain that the puppies were being given away? She swallowed. What would he tell her about why Penny wasn't around any longer? A lump formed in her throat. Tyler was a good father and even though thinking of him unleashed a ferocious pang of pain inside her, she hoped he and Rain would find their own happiness.

She whispered a prayer that Tyler's heart would heal, even as her own felt like it was falling into pieces.

On Penny's last official Friday, the officers ordered a massive goodbye cake and presented her with a bouquet of pink roses. Tyler wasn't sure he should attend the party after what he'd said to Penny, but he made up his mind to go, anyway. He would do his best not to make her feel any more uncomfortable than he already had.

Penny was dressed in civilian clothes—a soft pink sweater and slim brown pants—and her hair was tied in her favored loose ponytail. Two high spots of color stood out on her pale cheeks. For one moment, her gaze locked with his, but she quickly looked away. He took a seat at the far end of the conference room and tried to wear a pleasant expression.

She picked at her cake and offered rounds of smiles and hugs, but Tyler saw her blink back tears. He was ashamed of himself for adding to her pain, for his childish need to hurt her to vent his own wild sadness. After his outburst at the hotel, he'd spent time with Rain and in prayer. Nothing soothed the lancing anguish in his own heart. Hour upon hour, he'd paced the nights away, until exhaustion drove him to sleep. But something had clicked in those endless minutes—a tiny flame had ignited that showed him the truth.

Somewhere in those turbulent hours, he'd come to understand without any doubt that he'd let the scars of the past tether him. A failed marriage and Diane's abandonment hung around his heart like twin anchors, weighing down his soul in a way God had not intended. It shamed him to think of it, to consider how he'd unburdened that heaviness on a beautiful person like Penny.

Why hadn't he been stronger, like her? She'd soldiered on bravely in spite of what Randall had done to her and her family. She dared to see herself as a light in the world instead of a victim. Part of him knew deep down that she'd even perhaps considered stepping further away from that past and embracing something new when she'd reached out to him and Rain. Could there be any clearer example of courage than that? And his own fear had kept him from reaching back.

Breathing shallow, he thought about his plan. He did not know if he could undo the damage he'd caused with Penny. It was a good possibility that she would head to a new job and a new life no matter how eloquent his words, and he would never see her again. All he knew was he'd prayed fervently that morning for God to help him make things right between them. He needed time alone with her, but that proved to be a problem with a roomful of cops gathered around.

He'd offered to drive her back to the safe house, still her home for the uncertain future, and she'd declined, of course. Bradley had already volunteered for the job. Unbeknownst to her, he'd taken over the task from Bradley, anyway. He humbled himself and explained to Bradley what he was going to attempt.

"You sure you know what you're doing, Walker?" Bradley had said.

“No, but I’m going to give it my best shot to make up for how I’ve hurt her.”

“All right,” Bradley said with a wink.

Tyler felt suddenly nervous. “Got any advice?”

“Don’t say anything stupid.” He whacked Tyler on the shoulder and walked away smiling.

Tyler swallowed against the tightness in his throat. The ride would be his last chance to undo some of the damage he’d done to himself and to her. He prayed God would help him find the right words.

After the office goodbyes were done, Gavin was the last one to hug Penny. “You know that if you ever change your mind, you have a job here waiting.”

Penny kissed his cheek. “I appreciate that so much, Sarge.”

He touched her shoulder. “We’ll get Randall soon. Don’t send out that resume yet, okay? I’m still hoping we can change your mind.”

“I know you’ll catch Randall, but I think

it's time for me to start over somewhere new, without so many memories. It's better this way."

Tyler's heart cracked open a little wider.

Penny shouldered her tote bag and took Scrappy's leash. Bradley followed behind with King after they got the all-clear from the patrol officer outside.

Her eyes rounded. "I thought Bradley was taking me."

"I took over the assignment."

He could tell she wanted to ask why, but he wasn't prepared to tell her, not with Bradley right behind them.

"Move it, Walker. Quit slacking," Bradley said.

In spite of Bradley's forced cheer, Tyler saw Penny's pain mirrored in her brother's face. *And you probably were the final push in getting her to quit,* he thought miserably.

"Okay." Bradley held King's leash. "Meet you at the safe house. We can discuss your plan to go stay with your friend in Florida."

Tyler cleared his throat and opened the passenger-side door for Penny.

She kissed her brother on the cheek. "It's okay if you have work to do. We don't need to talk about it now." She opened the rear door to let Scrappy and Dusty into Tyler's back seat.

Bradley waved her off. "Nah. I've got a hankering for chow mein. I figured we could do takeout. That's..."

Tyler heard the screech of tires. In a blur of motion, a grey truck roared up the street. A squad car followed the speeding car—code three. The noise from the chase bounced off the walls of the police station and echoed along the narrow street.

He knew it was Randall behind the wheel, even before the truck jumped the curb and careened onto the sidewalk.

Penny screamed.

Bradley reached for his weapon, but he had no time to react. The truck's front bumper struck him with a sickening thud that sent him sailing backward onto the pavement. He landed in a limp heap. King avoided the collision, barking at a fever pitch. The truck slammed to a halt when it plowed into the back of Tyler's vehicle. Dusty and Scrappy launched themselves out of the car through the open door.

Penny's mouth was open in shock, her eyes riveted on her fallen brother. He was lying completely still, one arm flung above his head.

"Bradley," she shrieked, her voice almost unrecognizable. Tyler tried to pull her behind him as he reached for his revolver. She wrenched herself from Tyler's grasp and ran toward her brother. King was loose, barking and jumping in a frenzy. Frantically, he snatched at King's leash, hauling him back, while trying futilely to aim his revolver at the crumpled truck.

Just as he was ready to squeeze off a shot at the opening truck door, Penny crossed into the line of fire. He eased up and Randall seized the moment to dive from the truck. A gun flashed in his hand as he headed toward Penny and grabbed her by the wrist.

"Drop the weapon, Randall," Tyler hollered.

Tyler still could not risk taking a shot since Penny was between him and Randall. She was pulling and flailing at her captor.

King's barking reached ferocious levels as he lunged and jerked at the leash. He had a target now. Randall Gage, the man who had taken down his partner. If Tyler released King, would Randall shoot? A bullet at this range might kill Penny, Bradley or King.

Scrappy circled Penny, teeth snapping, as Randall wrapped his arm around her neck, gun pressed to her temple. Dusty barked at full volume, too, adding to the melee.

"Call off those dogs or I'm going to shoot her right here," Randall screamed.

Scrappy continued to yelp and bark. Randall shot wildly, the bullet plowing into Tyler's rear tire.

"Stay," Tyler thundered at the dogs. The command had no effect on King, but Dusty sat and, mercifully, Scrappy froze. He did not sit, but he stood in place, whining, the scruff on his neck raised like King's, every nerve in his body taut.

Randall jutted his chin at King. "Him, too. Call off the big one." Randall's green eyes were wide with fear and rage as he shouted over King's ferocious barking. Tyler felt as though King's yanking was about to dislocate his shoulder. Penny clutched at Randall's arm.

"He won't back down," Tyler yelled. "I'm not his handler."

"You get that dog away from me or she's dead." Randall dug the gun in hard, causing Penny to cry out.

"Okay," Tyler said. "Give me a minute. I'll secure him in the car."

Backing slowly, he dragged the frantic King back toward his vehicle. The dog fought him at every step. "See? We're doing what you want, Randall," Tyler called over his shoulder. "There's no reason to shoot again."

It took all his strength to march the dog back where he could clip his leash to a hook in the car. King thrashed and barked so loudly Tyler's eardrums vibrated. At least Dusty and Scrappy stayed put for the moment.

Sweat beaded on Tyler's forehead. Cops were streaming from the office now, moving as close as they could to provide support. Randall would soon be surrounded, his capture inevitable. Tyler knew he had only seconds before Randall would kill Penny as his final act of vengeance.

Back toward Randall, he noticed a piece of broken asphalt on the ground near his open car door. An idea sizzled through his brain. What he was going to do might instigate a bloodbath. Randall might be arrested, but he could take many lives before that happened, including Penny's. There was no more time to think it through.

Now or never, Walker.

In one fluid motion, he grabbed the chunk, turned and fired the rock as close to Randall's head as he could manage without hitting Penny. It caused Randall to flinch. At the same time, Scrappy launched himself at Randall, who staggered backward, the gun sailing from his hand. Quickly Tyler released King, who flew like a missile toward his partner's attacker and clamped onto his leg.

Randall screamed and batted at King and Scrappy.

"Stop resisting," Tyler shouted to Randall, but he continued to thrash and swear.

Penny fell and immediately scrambled up again. Sobbing, she staggered toward her brother. Scrappy turned and raced to her. She was yelling Bradley's name, lurching the last few feet to reach her brother. Bradley was still lying on his side, blood pooling around his head.

It took all of Tyler's will and repeated orders from Jackson to get King to release. Finally, the dog did so and Jackson took charge of him. King whined pitifully, trying to get to his fallen partner.

Henry secured the weapon and cuffed Randall.

"I should have killed Penny twenty years ago and then come back for her brother," Randall screamed.

Bathed in sweat, Tyler waved in the ambulance. A medic raced over and began work on Bradley as another saw to Randall's wounds. A ring of officers watched, horror on their faces, as Penny clutched her brother's hand, sobbing silently until Tyler gently pulled her away.

"I want to stay with him. Please..." she cried.

"We have to let the medics take care of

him now," Tyler said, holding her tightly so she could not run to her brother.

Bradley was loaded onto a stretcher and whisked into an ambulance. Tyler watched over Penny's shoulder. Bradley had still not moved at all, his face a stark white except where it was smeared with blood.

When the ambulance had departed, Tyler released Penny, but kept his arm around her. She remained on the sidewalk, gripping Tyler's arm, her body quaking with emotion. When Scrappy licked her face and she collapsed to her knees, Tyler kneeled next to her.

Her breath came in shuddery gasps. "My brother," she moaned over and over again. Tears poured down her pale face and her eyes were mirrors of grief and shock.

"Listen to me."

She trembled and would not look at him.

Tyler cupped her cheeks and gently tipped her face to his. "Penny, Bradley is alive. He's breathing on his own. Those are two good signs. The hospital will give him the best care, I promise."

She clasped his forearms and that shimmering caramel gaze met his for the first time in days. Tears clung to her long eyelashes like diamond chips. "Tyler, I'm scared. I'm so scared."

"I know. Me, too." And then he folded her in his arms and prayed soft and low, oblivious to the cops gathered all around, the red lights strobing, the whine of the dogs. He prayed with everything in him that Penny would not lose her brother. She nestled against him, shivering, crying, listening.

He had the dim sense that crowds were gathering, thrill seekers and passersby that stopped to discern what had just taken place. Looking up, he discovered that the Brooklyn K-9 officers had formed a tight circle around them, cops and their dogs, shielding Tyler and Penny from the curious glances. They stood shoulder-to-shoulder, protecting their own. His heart swelled.

Closing his eyes, he pressed Penny closer, hoping she could feel her police family gathered around her, praying that Randall Gage had not accomplished his deadly mission.

SIXTEEN

Penny and Scrappy walked the hospital hallways as the hours ticked by in agonizing slow motion. They were never alone. When she felt like talking, Tyler or Vivienne was there. When she simply wanted to cry, Gavin strolled along with her, handing over tissues and a bottle of water, or cups of weak hospital coffee. Jackson brought King, after he was checked out by the vet. The dog whined forlornly.

It was all terribly familiar. When Tyler had been brought here, she'd known him only slightly, a no-nonsense cop who thought her little more than a child. Now he stood next to her, tenderly anticipating her every need, his presence more comforting than she could have ever imagined. In the rare moments he'd left her side, she'd heard him quietly singing a song to Rain over the phone. It was an off-key version of the bus song she'd taught Rain. He didn't get very many of the words right, but the rhythm was perfect.

His words circled through the numbness in her mind.

I'm a single father and I shouldn't have let you become a part of our lives. I should have known you were going to leave us.

Yet he was caring for her now, but not the way she'd yearned for. It wasn't love, it was duty to Bradley, respect and care for a colleague's kin.

Not love.

It would not be that.

When they got the word that Bradley would be okay after he recovered from a concussion and two broken ribs, her knees buckled. All she could do was hold onto Scrappy's collar while he licked the tears that dripped from her chin and the officers crowded around her.

Randall Gage had not taken her brother away.

She thanked the Lord from the bottom of her heart, from the depths of her soul. Tyler stroked a hand across her back and pressed tissues in her palm. She saw that there were tears in the brilliant blue of his eyes, too.

"Randall is behind bars?" She said it to Tyler more to make it real in her mind than anything else.

"Yes, ma'am. And he's going to stay there forever. He'll never hurt you or Bradley or anyone else again."

"I can't even make myself believe it."

Gavin smiled. "You've had twenty years to worry. It may take some time for the truth to sink in."

She went silent. Tyler's fingers pressed comforting circles on her back as her hand stroked Scrappy's soft fur before he helped her to her feet and into a chair. She managed a watery smile. “Scrappy turned out to be a pretty big help, didn’t he? Not bad for a police school dropout”

Tyler smiled, but it faded quickly. His hands fell to his lap. “Penny, I know this isn’t the time, but…”

The door opened and the nurse appeared. “You can go in…” She hadn’t finished her sentence when King surged forward, yanking the leash out of Jackson’s hands, hurtling away to find Bradley.

Gavin went after him, apologizing to the startled nurse, and the cops laughed and broke into clusters for private conversations.

Penny followed Gavin, turning to look at Tyler. “What did you want to tell me?”

“It can wait,” he said. “Go on. Your brother needs you.”

She had to stop herself from running to Bradley’s room.

Her brother was going to be okay. Gavin was doing his best to hold back King, who was straining to leap onto the bed with

Bradley. Sarge finally succeeded in getting all four of King's paws back on the ground.

When she got a good look at Bradley, she nearly collapsed again. Gripping his bed rail, she pored over the face of her handsome brother. His head was muffled in bandages and his right eye was swollen shut. Tubes and monitors connected him to a variety of beeping machines.

"I'm going to take this big galoot out of here and let you two have a minute alone," Gavin said.

Penny nodded gratefully. She bent close to Bradley and gently touched his undamaged cheek. He smiled wanly and then grimaced.

"Hurts to smile."

"I'm sorry. I'm so sorry."

He raised the hand that was free of the IV. She clasped it, tears flowing freely. "Sarge told me they made the arrest. It's finally over, sis."

She had to bend to hear him. Over.

Could it possibly be true? "I can't wrap my mind around it. All I care about is that you're going to be okay."

"I am...and so are you. We can start over now. Randall is out of our lives."

She swallowed hard, trying to make it real.

"So you don't have to quit," he croaked.

She didn't have to because of Randall, but there was still the mess in her heart left over from what had happened with Tyler. It was not going to be possible to see him every day at work, watch his little daughter grow right before her eyes, witness daily what she could not be a part of.

She reached over and kissed her brother gently as his eyes started to close.

"Rest now. We can talk about this later."

When his breathing relaxed into a regular rhythm, she said a prayer of profound gratitude that the Lord had spared her brother.

On Bradley's third day in the hospital, Tyler went to see him, smuggling in a plate of his mother's lasagna.

"Oh, man," Bradley said, sitting up, "am I ready for real food."

"That's a good sign." It was also a good sign that his bruises were starting to fade slightly. The cuts on his arm were scabbing over, as well.

"How's King doing with Jackson?"

"Jackson's been taking him to the office with him and every morning he runs to your cubicle expecting to find you there. Jackson says he's cranky, pure and simple."

"Aww. He's the best partner."

"Next best thing to a golden retriever."

"In your dreams." He peeled back a corner of the foil-covered plate and inhaled. "Your mom is a culinary genius."

"I'll tell her you said that." They made small talk until Tyler shifted and cleared his throat. "I've been thinking."

Bradley looked up from his perusal of the lasagna. "Yeah? About what?"

"About the question you asked me before." Tyler swallowed. "About what Penny means to me."

Bradley set aside the plate and folded his hands across the blanket. "And what is your answer to that question?"

He took a deep breath and let it out slowly. Time to make it all real. "She means everything to me, and I want her to be in my life forever." Breath held, he waited to see how Bradley would react.

For a moment, Bradley's face seemed to be made of stone. Slowly a smile replaced the scowl. "Well, it's about time, Tyler the Timid. The guy who gets Penny is going to be the most fortunate man in the universe and you almost let her get away, you big dope." He rolled his eyes. "I thought I was going to have to knock some sense into you."

Tyler felt his whole body relax. "So you think I'm worthy of her?"

"Not by a long shot, but you can spend the rest of your life trying to be worthy of her." He grinned. "And that means taking care of her brother, too. You know, bending to my every whim, bringing me fresh-squeezed orange juice and giving me your parking place."

Tyler let him go on awhile. "But what if I can't change her mind?"

Bradley rolled his eyes. "Then I guess you aren't trying hard enough. What are you doing wasting time here? Get on it, Detective. She's planning on sticking around until I'm on my feet again, but after that, she'll split unless you change her mind."

There was a knock on the door and a slim blonde lady popped her head in. "May I come in?"

Tyler raised an eyebrow as Bradley straightened and sat up higher on the bed. "I don't know if Officer McGregor is up for visitors," Tyler said.

"I'm Sasha Eastman. I work for a local news station and I want to do an interview with Bradley and Penny McGregor."

Tyler thought Bradley looked a bit crestfallen that the beautiful lady had an agenda. "A reporter?" he said. "No thanks. You called the office already and we declined."

She smiled. "And you avoided my call, too. I never even got to speak to you."

Bradley's cheeks flushed. "I'm not interested in providing an interview."

"You haven't heard the whole idea. I want to do a show about your parents' murders."

"No thanks. My sister and I learned a long time ago that we don't talk to reporters."

"I'm not your run-of-the-mill reporter, Mr. McGregor." Her smile was warm and gentle. "I believe by telling your story we can draw out information about the copycat killer. Maybe even help you make an arrest."

Bradley frowned. "Like I said, Penny and I don't talk to reporters. Sorry."

Tyler took that as his cue. "I'll walk you to the elevator, Ms. Eastman. Thanks for stopping by."

"All right." She laid a business card on

Bradley's table. "But I'm a pretty determined lady. I think we'll be seeing each other again."

Bradley didn't answer as Tyler led Sasha out of the room. Before the door closed, he turned back to Bradley.

"Do you want me to ask her to bring your fresh-squeezed orange juice? She's way better looking than I am."

A balled-up paper napkin hit the door as it closed on Tyler's chuckling.

Penny breathed in the pure joy of being back in their Sheepshead Bay home. She steeped herself in the pleasure of tending to her struggling plants and cleaning out the fridge before she restocked it with Bradley's favorites. She'd tackled the cooking by storm, first baking Bradley's favorite blueberry muffins, then working her way on to a pot of beef stew and even firing up the bread machine with a loaf of herbed Italian bread. Bradley's appetite had not yet fully returned, but she was determined to change that. Each day she produced a new batch of his favorites, surreptitiously sliding a portion into the freezer for him to eat later.

Then she set about refreshing the old house with vases full of fall mums, a fat scented candle for the tiny kitchen table and a fall-patterned kerchief for Scrappy. Each and every detail brought her both pain and pleasure, when she considered her future.

Penny figured on delaying her start with the new K-9 unit another month while Bradley settled into his three weeks of recuperation leave. They had graciously agreed to give her all the time she needed to tend to him. She was Bradley's self-appointed chef and errand runner, but when Bradley returned to full strength, she intended to make some changes. He was not adjusting well to lying around. King, on the other hand, seemed perfectly content to sprawl on the floor at Bradley's feet, snoring or watching basketball on the big-screen TV. Scrappy occupied a spot on the other side of the room, enjoying a beam of fall sunshine.

"You don't have to quit," Bradley had said again just that morning.

"I feel like it's the right thing to do." He'd pressed her for a reason, but she'd changed the subject. It was too difficult to explain to her brother all that was going on inside her heart and mind.

Though she was devastated at leaving her Brooklyn K-9 Unit family, she knew it was time to start a new chapter on her own. Randall had finally been excised from their lives. She'd survived his horrors and come out stronger. It would be good for Bradley, too, to restart his life without his sister always hovering nearby.

A fresh start…a new life. Why did her stomach squeeze when she considered it?

Because she had been afraid for so long that she didn't know what to do now that she wasn't.

Or was it the real reason, which she

would not admit even to her brother...? Tyler. He'd made it clear that he regretted the feelings he had for her and that left a hurt that would not dissipate. How could she work at the same office with him? See him and Rain on a regular basis and not mourn the love she had for them?

Love—it was the correct word. It floored her to think it, but she had fallen in love with a man who didn't want her. When tears pricked her eyes, she straightened her shoulders. Soon it would be all over and the memories would recede into the past, where they would not hurt so much.

"There's nothing on TV," Bradley said now. "Why can't I take King for a walk?"

"Because the doctor said you're supposed to lie down and rest."

He rolled his eyes. "How does he know what's good for me?"

"Because he has a degree in medicine. You, on the other hand, believe that an ACE bandage can fix everything from a broken arm to sudden organ failure."

"ACE bandages are very versatile," he grumbled, watching her walk toward the hall closet. "Where are you going?"

She shouldered her bag. "To Coney Island. Rain is having a birthday party and she invited me to come. Just a casual thing." She was still feeling all kinds of awkward around Tyler, but she figured a birthday party would hold enough distraction to keep her from having to make conversation with him. She tucked the neatly wrapped present into her bag.

"A birthday party? I wanna go." He made a move to sit up. "I'll just sit quietly with King and…"

She pointed a finger at him until he sank down again. "You'll do no such thing. I will be back in a couple of hours and if there is cake, I will bring you a piece if you're very well behaved."

He groaned, and she walked back and kissed him on the forehead. "You're a real drill sergeant."

"A drill sergeant who loves her brother."

She stroked his hair. Tears welled in her eyes when she recalled him sprawled on the sidewalk, plowed down by Randall's car.

He caught her hand. "I love you, too, sis. Have a good time."

She rubbed Scrappy's ears and clipped on his leash. When she reached for the window to peek out through the curtains, she caught herself. Randall was in jail and that's where he would stay. She had her life back.

Bradley was looking at her. "Go on," he said softly, as if he understood exactly.

She blew him a kiss.

Though her insides were jittery at the prospect of seeing Tyler again, she was still wrapped in gratitude that her brother was safe and sound. Straightening her shoulders, she headed for the door.

SEVENTEEN

Scrappy watched avidly out the window as they drove to Coney Island. It didn't matter if they were going to the beach or the Laundromat. Scrappy was her ever-eager assistant. "You're always ready to go anywhere with me, aren't you?" Her gratitude toward Gavin for allowing her to formally adopt Scrappy was boundless. The dog was her devoted companion and no matter where life took her, he would always be right by her side, a treasured part of her family. Along the way, she caught herself glancing in the rearview mirror every so often.

Randall's gone, she repeated to herself. She wondered how long it would take her to fully believe it. Maybe the new job in Bronx would erase the lingering memories.

She parked and walked Scrappy along the boardwalk to Nathan's Famous hot dogs, where Tyler stood with one hand holding Dusty's leash and the other wrapped around Rain's little fingers. When Rain saw Penny, she broke away and ran to her. Penny scooped her up.

"Happy birthday, big girl."

Rain carefully held up each of her pointer fingers.

"Two years old? Wow." Penny kissed her on the cheek and eyed Tyler uneasily. "Where are the guests? Am I early?"

"You are the only guest she wanted to invite."

Her cheeks flooded with heat. "Oh. Well, you didn't have to do that. I could have dropped a present by your house. No need to—"

"I wanted to see you, too."

He had? Why? she wanted to ask, but he continued.

"I'll just get us some hot dogs. Do you two want to find a bench to sit on?"

Penny hesitated. The last time she'd been in charge of Rain, the child had disappeared. Cold rippled through her along with the October breeze. "I..."

He nodded firmly. "We can sit and eat our hot dogs and watch the surf." He held up a plastic bucket and shovel. "I promised her we would make a sand castle."

She swallowed and took Rain's hand and the plastic bucket. "All right." She and Rain settled on a metal bench, where they could look out on the wide stretch of sandy beach.

"Castle?" Rain said.

"Yes, Daddy says we are going to build a castle right after lunch."

Rain occupied herself watching the seagulls that swooped down toward the foamy waves. Scrappy tracked their progress, too, his whiskers twitching.

Tyler returned and put Dusty into a sit. He handed Penny a hot dog with mustard only. "Bradley said you're a purist, a mustard-only kind of gal."

She wondered why Tyler and her brother had been discussing her condiment choices.

His hot dog was loaded with every condiment that would fit, and a third plate held a hot dog sliced into small pieces with a puddle of ketchup for dipping.

Rain happily began to eat her hot dog slices. Penny nibbled at her own lunch, wondering why Tyler had arranged for her to be a private guest at Rain's party. Surely Francine had wanted to come.

"I wanted to talk to you," Tyler said, after a bite of his messy hot dog. "But you've been hard to find lately."

"I've been on nursing duty."

"How's Bradley as a patient?"

"The worst. I've been tempted to handcuff him to get him to keep still."

Tyler laughed. "Not surprised. He wants to get back to work to track down the Emerys' killer now that Randall is headed to prison." He went quiet for a moment. "Penny, what I want to talk to you about is..."

At that moment, Rain suddenly pointed to a seagull flapping nearby. Her gesture collided with Tyler's hot dog and it splatted directly against his chest with a messy squelch.

He jumped up, dropping the hot dog and knocking over Rain's lunch. A seagull swooped in and snatched away Tyler's fallen food. Scrappy gulped up Rain's.

"Oh, Scrappy," Penny chided.

The dog didn't look the slightest bit guilty as he swiped a tongue across his fleshy lips.

Rain began to cry. Tyler dabbed at the colorful mess staining his long-sleeved navy shirt.

"I'll run and get more napkins." Penny jogged to grab a handful from the restaurant and, when she returned, Rain had already stopped crying, and was clutching her bucket.

"Castle," she insisted.

Tyler took the extra napkins and managed to wipe off most of the debris, but the mustard and relish had left a wide smear across his chest. He surveyed the damage. "That looked much better on my hot dog than on my shirt."

"Messy," Rain said.

Penny smothered a grin.

Tyler nodded ruefully. "Yep, that's messy all right. Well, I guess I'm done with my lunch."

"You can have mine," Penny said, handing over her hot dog. "I'm full, anyway, and it looks like Rain doesn't want anymore."

Tyler gratefully accepted and finished her hot dog in two bites before they walked down to the sand.

They watched the rolling waves for a few minutes, while Dusty and Scrappy sniffed the landscape. Rain started to fill her bucket with dry sand. When she dumped it out, she grew perplexed that the sand did not stick together.

"We need some wet stuff," said Tyler. "I'll get it." He took the little yellow bucket and moved toward the surf. A couple of shovel scoops and he had filled it. As he stood up with a grin on his face, Dusty barked at a nearby seagull. Both dogs raced after the bird, so close to Tyler that he stumbled back a pace, stepping into the hole he'd just made in the sand. He went down on his backside, just as a wave rolled in from the ocean. His shoulders contracted as a foamy crest of water doused him completely.

Penny clapped a hand to her mouth as he sprang up, soaking wet and blinking.

"Oo-o-o-hhh," Rain said. "Wet."

Tyler retrieved the bucket and shovel, then returned to the dry sand. "Here you go," he said to Rain with a completely straight face, handing over the bucket. "I can guarantee this is the wet stuff."

Rain happily took the sand and dumped

it out. Then she set to work refilling the bucket, completely absorbed in her task.

Tyler looked so comical standing there with his clothes soaked and the stain of condiments on his shirt that Penny started to giggle.

"I'm sorry," she said. "I shouldn't laugh, but…"

He chuckled. "That's okay. This hasn't exactly gone like I planned."

Both of them began to laugh outright until their merriment died away.

"Rain doesn't seem to mind the birthday mess," Penny said.

"Her birthday is actually Monday and she's bringing cupcakes to her tiny tot class. Today's celebration was just a reason to get you to come out with me."

She looked at him, puzzled. "Why did you want me to meet you?"

He drew close and held his hand out. "I'm waterlogged and messy, but I have something important to say and I'm going to say it, even though nothing has gone right today."

Heart beating fast at the intensity of his eyes, she took his hand. His fingers were cold and sandy. Automatically, she pressed them between hers and tried to rub some warmth back in them. He stared at their joined hands as if he saw something incredible there.

"This is why," he said.

"Why what?"

He raised her hand in his. "This right here. The way you offer comfort to everyone, the way you nurture and love. It's in your DNA, it's who you are."

She stared. "I… I'm not sure."

"I'm sure. More sure than anything else I've ever known. Penny, you are a one in a million."

She blushed and tried to move her hands away, but he grabbed them.

"And I love you."

Her eyes went wide. "But…"

"I love you. I was afraid to say it because of my past failures. I mean, look…" He surveyed his shirt, gritty with mustard and sand. "I planned this perfect romantic situation so I could tell you that and this is how it turned out. But it's okay. If every plan I make in the future goes bust… I can live with that, as long as you're with me."

Shivers erupted up and down her spine. "The things you said…"

"Were untrue. I wanted to blame you for leaving me, but that wasn't your fault, it was mine. I've been dillydallying around, too scared to tell you how important you are to me. Tyler the Timid."

She raised an eyebrow. "Where'd you come up with that?"

"Your brother's nickname for me, but he's right." He pulled her closer. "I'm done being timid. I'm going to lay it all out there and tell you that I want you to stay at the office, in Brooklyn, with me. I want to marry you. I want us to be a family."

It was hard for her to believe it could be true. This man, the man who would not leave her thoughts, was offering her a life with him, the future that she'd always wanted. Her gaze traveled from his riveting blue eyes to Rain. "I'm not… I mean, I don't know how good a mother I would be to Rain."

"Look at me, Penny."

She dragged her eyes back to his face, lower lip between her teeth.

"Do you love me? Can you love me now that you know what a…" He looked at his shirt again. "What a mess I can be? After I hurt you and pushed you away? Do you love me?"

Tears blurred her vision. "Yes," she whispered. "I do, and I love Rain, too."

He gulped audibly. "Do you love us enough to step into this messy life with me and my daughter? I can't say it will be smooth sailing. As a matter of fact, I'm sure it won't. But I can promise you that I will love you every day of my life and I will try to be worthy of the amazing woman that you are."

She looked out at the waves, so much less vivid than his eyes. Rain dumped her bucket and started over. Penny took in the intensity of her knitted brow, so like her father's as, she began again on a new structure, better and stronger than the one she'd built before. When Penny looked at Tyler again, he was on one knee, holding a velvet box that held a slender gold band with a glittering, square-cut, pink diamond.

"Not a plain diamond, not for you. It's not good enough, I'm not good enough, but I'm asking you to accept it. Will you marry me?"

"Yes," she whispered as he slid the ring onto her finger. "I love you, Tyler."

"I love you, too, Penny."

Scrappy barked and he and Dusty raced again to the edge of the surf. Rain upended the bucket and clapped as the lopsided sand castle stood strong.

Tyler grabbed Penny up in a hug, twirling her around, sand flying, his wet shirt dampening her jacket, the scent of mustard and relish clinging to him. As he kissed her, she knew her life would be here in Brooklyn with her police family, her brother and Scrappy, and Tyler and Rain, the family God had put in her path to teach her how to love like Him.

* * * * *

Look for Bradley MacGregor's story,
Delayed Justice *by Shirlee McCoy,*
the next book in the True Blue K-9 Unit: Brooklyn series available in November 2020
from Love Inspired Suspense.

Dear Reader,

Dogs are amazing, aren't they? While I don't have a stellar police K-9 like Dusty, I do enjoy the company of a fuzzy little rescue dog named Junie. She's ten pounds of trouble in a fur coat! Like Scrappy, she doesn't quite hit the mark in terms of obedience. We love her nonetheless. Junie is to us, what Scrappy is to Penny—unconditional love and commitment. It was so sweet to be able to give poor Penny a canine companion. She has endured such difficulty in her life and she struggles to see herself the way God sees her. I think we all feel like that from time to time. I hope you remember when you are feeling like that, that you are lovable because God says you are. He made you, dear friends, and He doesn't want our hurts and disappointments to cause us to forget that.

Thank you for coming along on this continuity series with me. I hope you found the book to be a blessing. If you'd like to connect further, you can reach me via my website at www.danamentink.com. There is also a physical address there if you prefer to correspond by mail.

God bless you!
Dana Mentink